TAKE ME TO THE LAKE

Sophia Nicole

Grosvenor House
Publishing Limited

The right of Sophia Nicole to be identified as the author of this
work has been asserted in accordance with Section 78
of the Copyright, Designs and Patents Act 1988

The book cover is copyright to Sophia Nicole
Cover image copyright to Dace Znotina

This book is published by
Grosvenor House Publishing Ltd
Link House
140 The Broadway, Tolworth, Surrey, KT6 7HT.
www.grosvenorhousepublishing.co.uk

This book is a work of fiction. Any resemblance to
people or events, past or present, is purely coincidental.

A CIP record for this book
is available from the British Library

ISBN 978-1-80381-176-5
eBook ISBN 978-1-80381-177-2

For Mum and Dad

You blessed me with wings and encouraged me
to soar, teaching me the sky is the limit,
and for that, I am grateful.

Preface

Writing has always been a passion of mine. When I was little, I would write down anything my imagination came up with, whether it was a short story, characters and their backgrounds, or just a different universe entirely. I especially enjoyed writing poetry, and when I took part in a competition through my primary school to write a poem about bullying, I used my experiences of being a victim of it to write a piece. I never thought I would win the competition at only nine years old and get to have it published in a book with other winners throughout the country, or two years later to have another poem published, this one written about homelessness.

It was only as I got into my teens that I decided to have a go at writing a novel in the six-week holidays, but once I'd written it, I didn't think to do much with it other than be proud of myself for drafting a whole novel. I wasn't the most confident of teenagers, so the thought of showing what I'd written to anyone was enough to make me run for the hills.

Years went by, and in my twenties, life took me down a path of some sort that I wasn't expecting it to, an emotional rollercoaster I wasn't prepared for, with plenty of twists and turns. I had many feelings that I'd never experienced before and didn't know how to make sense of them. I decided that the best way to deal with these emotions was to put pen to paper, so I did, but instead of just writing how I felt, I chose to create a character who could feel my emotions for me.

Coral, the main character in the novel, had different reasons for feeling the emotions she experienced, and she reacted to them in different ways than I did. The situations messing with her emotions were not like mine, but being able to describe them in such a creative way spurred me on to do so much more than just write about one character and how she felt. Instead, I created a whole world surrounding this character with a mystery to solve and so much more than I expected from the start.

In the end, years later, after starting and stopping my writing of this novel, I found myself again. I was on a much clearer path and had finally found a way out of the darkness, and I was able to finish the novel, and finally had the confidence to show it to the world.

So, in a sense, this book is to show people that no matter what darkness you may find yourself in and how tough situations may be in your life, it's not forever; you can find a way out and back into the light again, no matter how long it takes.

Acknowledgements

Thank you to Grosvenor House Publishing for giving me the opportunity to make my dream of becoming an author a reality. Everyone at Grosvenor House Publishing has been so welcoming from the very first day, willing to help in any way they can, and providing all the help and positivity I could ask for. Also, a huge thank you to Melanie for all you have done – you put my mind at ease throughout the process and have been so forthcoming with giving advice and support along the way.

Thank you to my mum and dad for bringing me up to know that the sky is the limit, and that if I put my mind to anything, then I can do it. Especially that no matter how many hurdles get in my way, anything is possible; there's no such word as can't when it comes to wanting to achieve my dreams.

I also have huge gratitude to everyone who has supported me over the years, whether that be back in my teenage years or throughout my twenties – your love and support has never gone unnoticed, and you've helped me get back on my feet in more ways than I can list. It's helped me to become the woman I am today.

Above all else, thank you to every author of every book that I've ever had the privilege to read and get sucked into the world they have created, never having the strength to put the book down and stop reading. Books have always accumulated in my bedroom, and they will continue to do so. I will always be a bookworm, and that's because of the immensely brilliant authors out there who I've grown to love from childhood to adulthood – a constant inspiration for the creative imagination I will continue to let flourish. You let childhood Sophia explore many worlds, with many characters and many stories, and that will always hold steady in my heart, and will continue to do so throughout every book I get to lay my eyes on and delve into.

1

Coral frantically scanned the road outside the sixth form block of her school, and a sudden rush of relief consumed her as she spotted her best friend's pickup truck. Charging across the road like a rhino, despite oncoming cars, she swiftly opened the truck door, slid through the gap and hopped in, throwing her bag into the back.

"Go, Iris, go," she shouted, forcefully slapping her hands down onto the dashboard. Iris put the vehicle into gear and sped off down the road, dodging out of the way of a car pulling out of the school gates, blasting their horn in disgust at her sudden burst into the road.

"What happened?" Iris asked in a panicked tone, checking the road behind them as her eyes darted from the road to the rear-view mirror like a scared animal would in a heightened chase. Coral didn't answer, her mind elsewhere, thinking about what she would do tonight. Probably the usual; blasting music and knocking back unlimited amounts of vodka or whiskey, which she'd always kept hidden under her bed, or maybe she'd roll a few spliffs and see what happened...

Pain suddenly shot through Coral's arm, disrupting her thoughts and returning her to the current situation of present life.

"Ouch!" she shrieked. "Why did you nip me?" she asked, rubbing her arm and looking at Iris, sending piercing daggers her way.

"Because you're having me drive like a lunatic, and you're not explaining why! Are we being chased? Did you piss someone off?"

Coral smiled to herself. "Well, *I* was getting chased, and I most definitely pissed someone off; I was due to have detention with Mr Rowland and had to make a run for it. It's not like he could've caught up with me anyway; he walks like he's shit himself most of the time. It's Friday. No way was I staying behind to listen to him ramble on and on."

Iris looked at her for a split second with absolute fire in her eyes before returning her focus to the road. "I can't *believe* you made us nearly crash because *you* chose to skip detention. You need to get back on track, Coral, it's getting ridiculous now, and you're nearly at the end of sixth form. It's almost the start of real life outside of the school gates for you; you need to wake up and realise this."

Coral sighed, rolling up the sleeves on her hoodie and turning her gaze to Iris with the best puppy dog eyes she could muster up.

"Take me to the lake."

That was the famous sentence of Coral Bayles. She would forever use this five-word sentence to free herself of life, and the only person who could ever bring her to her freedom was Iris, her Latina bombshell of a best friend. She always knew what Coral needed, whether it was booze, good music or an escape in the truck on the open road. However, Iris also gave her plenty of life advice, trying her best to keep her on the straight and narrow, but Coral knew she was too deep in, to the point of no return and had been for a long time. *We can't all be perfect*, she thought. *It would take way more effort to be perfect anyway, and who has time for that?*

From when Coral was in single figures of age, right up to before she was a teenager, Iris and Kruze, Coral's brother, had been friends for years. They'd worked on homework projects together for their ICT and business class, creating joint PowerPoint presentations and revising for exams with each other; that was how Coral and Iris's long-lasting friendship began. Once, when Iris came over to study with Kruze, there stood twelve-year-old Coral, innocent and willing to make a new friend out of Iris, no matter the age gap. She'd waited years to pluck up the courage to ask her without being embarrassed, watching Iris and Kruze in awe of the friendship they had, but Iris thought Coral was sweet and could tell she looked up to her, so she took that on board and helped Coral through every milestone she hit, or tried to at least. She was the older sister Coral never had, in a sense, in more ways than one.

Coral continued to stare out of the window as Iris drove them on the long winding roads until she pulled into the lay-by and turned off the engine. Luckily, there weren't many cars parked up in the afternoon sun, and as Coral hopped out of the truck, stretching her legs, she could just see in the distance a few dog walkers and a couple who were walking hand in hand. She took a deep breath and smiled to herself; being outdoors was something Coral loved doing the most. Right back from when she was a child, the fresh air filling her lungs made her feel more alive than anything as if she were an eagle ready to take flight or a wolf ready to howl and run with its pack; in those moments, it felt so much easier to breathe.

Iris joined her at the front of the truck, and they took the dirt path together, walking down through the trees to the water's edge. Coral wriggled out of her hoodie and tied it lazily around her waist, causing the sudden change in temperature to make her skin feel less clammy. As their pace slowed at the sight of the end of the dirt path, they both stood looking out across at the exquisite scene in front of them; the sun glinting off of the water as if beneath the shimmering depths lay glittering crystals waiting to be discovered.

Iris crossed her arms over her chest, not in a self-conscious way trying to hide away from the world, because that wasn't how Iris thought of herself, but instead, Coral could see it was most likely from feeling awkward at where they were stood.

"I still don't know how you do it," Iris said in a low voice, now looking at the ground, kicking away a few twigs and stones by her feet. Coral turned to her, trying her best to force a smile at her best friend but struggling ever so slightly.

"Do what?" she asked, even though she knew full well what it was that she meant. Sometimes she just wanted to hear it. It made it feel quite real at times, as if she needed reminding it wasn't just a bad dream she once had, but instead the grotesque reality she lived and breathed every single day.

"You know... coming to the lake after... what happened here."

Coral turned away and looked out at the lake in front of her. Such a beautiful place full of such sorrow, but only if Coral allowed it to feel that way, which she tried extremely hard not to do on a regular basis. That's what the alcohol and drugs were for, to drown it out and surround her like a comfort blanket.

"Well, the lake holds more good memories than bad ones for me," she said, cupping her hands over her eyes as the sun edged its way from behind a tree ever so slightly. "Plus, the lake parties here are immense, so I definitely can't miss out on those, can I?"

Iris smiled at Coral, but she could still sense the haunted look in her eyes.

Coral knew that everyone was aware of the lake and its ghost stories, especially hers, but she did her best to ignore it and block it out. Either that, or she'd end up back in the base of the black hole that once engulfed her years ago, and she wasn't sure if she'd be able to climb the slick black walls of it this time without giving up completely.

Taking a moment to think, she realised she was only halfway out of this bad place she'd mentally been in for years. Coral tried to convince herself she was fully out of it, but she knew even saying halfway out was beyond an exaggeration. This black hole in her mind and chest always reminded her of the rabbit hole from *Alice in Wonderland*, but instead of falling down it and ending up in Wonderland, Coral ended up in pure torturous hell. Maybe one day, she wouldn't have to convince herself anymore, and it would be a complete truth of her progress that she was out of the black hole and back into the fresh, vibrant, colourful world everyone else seemed to live in. Maybe one day she'd be truly at ease with her life.

I can wish and hope, Coral thought.

Iris cleared her throat, completely interrupting Coral from her thoughts and said, "Are you even listening to me?"

Coral shook her head, completely having lost track of what Iris had even said in the first place.

"I agreed with you; you can't miss out on the lake parties, and neither can I," Iris said, draping an arm over Coral's shoulders. Iris squeezed her shoulder and said, "Speaking of, how do you feel about engagements?"

Coral raised an eyebrow at Iris and smirked, pleased with the change of topic, suddenly feeling the sensation that her body was relaxing a little. "Listen, Iris, if that was your way of proposing to me, I'll have to pass. I mean, the lake is a good scenic place to do it, but I like the idea of someone getting down on one knee for me."

Iris smirked back at her and said, "That doesn't surprise me. We all know about you getting down on one knee yourself, or maybe both knees," and to that, Coral leant away, pulling an exaggerated half shocked face while laughing and lightly punched her friend in the arm. Iris started laughing too; any fragments of the negative vibes that were there between them moments ago had now fluttered away in the breeze. "Anyway, I don't know if you remember a jockstrap jack-off of a guy I knew at school?"

Coral stretched her arms above her head, saying, "I'll need more than that, Iris. There's a whole list that comes under that sort of description."

"Mason; he was in mine and Kruze's business class. Anyway, so he's now engaged to his girlfriend Brianna, and because I've been such a good neighbour to Bri-Bri over the years, I got an invite, including a plus one. So, if you don't mind having to drink a hefty load of alcohol at a lakeside party with yours truly, then you are more than welcome to be my date tomorrow night."

Coral grinned and launched herself at Iris, wrapping her arms around her. "This is one of the many reasons why I love being your best friend; you understand my destructive needs completely."

* * * *

After Coral and Iris had spent a handful of hours by the lake, talking about a range of things, laughing and joking until the sun had dipped enough for them to call it a day, she dropped Coral off back home. Coral looked up at her little house as she heard Iris pull away from the pavement; the dull early evening sky that circled above it that always seemed to be there was getting darker by the second. No matter how sunny a day it had been, it always seemed gloomy above her house. Suddenly, all the positive vibes she had from her and Iris' sing-along on the way home were quickly vacuumed away and replaced with a pang of cold dullness.

Coral's home used to be the one people talked about in the best way; the one where even if they only caught a glimpse, they'd instantly get a good sense of knowing it was full of happiness and love inside, just as it showed on the outside. It was always kept pristine, both inside and out, and the garden was always immaculate, full of arrays of flowers to brighten any day. People would come over just to say hello, to admire what had caught their eye and would be so hopeful of an invitation to come in and see just how beautiful the inside could be, if it was anything to go by from what they'd witnessed outside of the house. *Who'd have thought one person leaving could have such an effect on the remaining family and its surroundings*, Coral thought.

As Coral reached the front door, she placed her forehead against it and closed her eyes, feeling the coldness of the glass seep through her skin to her mind, merging itself with the icy darkness that had made a home in there already. She always struggled the most at home; even with her family around her, it still felt dysfunctional and broken beyond compare. The home that was once full of life now felt like an empty carcass.

If she had enough money, she'd most likely get her own place with her boyfriend Dylan and escape fully, but she knew she couldn't, and as much as she despised the thought, she did have to get through the rest of her final weeks of sixth form, as Iris kept reminding her. She could almost picture her friend now, looking at her with both sympathy and sternness, saying *failing isn't an option if you want a future*. But that was the thing; Coral wasn't sure if she did want a future.

Using the last segment of energy that she could muster, Coral made her way through the front door, and as she closed the door behind her, Kruze walked into the hallway, alerted by the only sound in the eerily quiet house. He gave a tired smile in her direction before looking in the hallway mirror.

"How was school?" he asked her, fixing up his uniform, looking as smart and nerdy as ever. Having a brother in the police force instantly made Coral feel that little bit safer, but she did worry that he overworked himself most days. Not that there was any need for it to feel safer than it was; there wasn't much chance someone would break into their house, unless someone had a way of stealing emotions. If that was the case, she'd open the door and happily invite them in to steal away every last speck of sadness and anger and let them take it all with them to dispose of somewhere far away from here.

At first, it was a lot to take in every day, breathing in the cold gloom that haunted the house, sticking to the walls and burrowing into every nook and cranny. But so many years had passed that the cold feeling had become normal room temperature to her; to them all, so much so they hardly even noticed it still lingered, completely numb to it. Probably because it was the only choice they had, accepting it was here to stay.

"It was fantastic. I love it so much that I *might* even consider extra classes after school, just for the fun of learning more," Coral said, looking deadly serious. Kruze rolled his eyes.

"If you continue with that sarcasm, you'll end up there permanently till you're in your twenties and not for the *fun of it*, as you say. Have you got any homework you need to do tonight?"

Coral simmered down and crossed her arms across her chest. "Kruze, it's sixth form, not school; I'm not 16, you know?"

"Yes, I know you're not. You're almost a fully functioning eighteen-year-old adult about to head into the real world of getting a job and working hard to pay bills. Now answer the question: have you got any homework you need to do tonight?"

Coral sighed. "I've got some coursework to do. It's nothing major, though, so don't worry, I'll get it done; scout's honour."

Kruze smiled gently, his eyes forever looking tired and worried. Providing for their family took everything out of him, and she knew that, so no wonder he could hardly sleep at night. Running a household was tough, and she tried her best to make it easy for Kruze, but she couldn't help but lash out when she didn't fully understand situations with money and other problems within their home.

She wanted to get a Saturday job to help out, but she knew doing sixth form five days a week and a Saturday job would be too much for her dishevelled brain to handle. Coral didn't really understand anything within her home or how it was still standing; she only just managed to keep herself alive and ticking over, let alone the roof over their heads.

"Well, if you need any help, just save it for tomorrow and I'll lend a hand," he said as he shoved his phone into a pocket of his backpack. Coral pulled a confused face, finally clicking in her head that seeing him in his uniform was unusual for a Friday evening.

"You're working tonight?" Coral asked. Usually, she'd find him sitting in front of the television with snacks and a few cans on the coffee table, encouraging her to watch unsolved murder cases or murder mystery films with him. It was one of the only things they enjoyed doing together, and even then they'd argue sometimes about the way the police were working on investigations. Kruze would always stick to the facts like he would at work, whereas Coral would go into more depth, really trying to pick apart each suspect, wishing *she* had them in the interrogation chair and was putting them through their paces.

"Yeah, I'm getting some extra hours in so we can afford to eat next month," he said and smirked at her, clearly finding himself funny. "Don't worry, though; I'll make sure to get enough money to afford your tortilla chips and dip."

Coral smiled to herself as he closed the door behind him. It didn't matter how much Kruze and Coral didn't get on at times, she would always have the utmost respect for him and how hard he worked to provide for them all. His dream of becoming a millionaire businessman had been boxed away years ago, and in its place was the dream to work for those who lived in his community and make a difference somehow, keeping them safe and alive. But the dream became more of an obsession when he was driven more by the previous years' events.

Coral threw her bag down by the sparse coat rack and made a move towards the kitchen. She poured herself a glass of warm grapefruit juice from the carton she'd accidentally left out this morning and leant against the worktop. After all the years that had passed by, she could never get used to how quiet and lifeless the house felt. How empty and lonely, like it was in a whole different universe of its own, making her skin crawl. She could spend a whole day out and about, having the time of her life, but the minute she stepped into her house, the emptiness filled her lungs and made it hard to breathe or even want to live, suffocating her completely. The darkness always found its way back into the front of her mind eventually; she just had to hope there was someone around when it did to keep her from becoming numb to its grasp on her and falling apart again.

Once she had finished her juice, she exited the kitchen and climbed up to the top of the wooden stairs, her bedroom door directly in front of her. She briefly turned to her right, peering over at the door that never seemed to open. Not seeing her dad often was something she'd had to quickly get used to, and even then, it never got any easier. She hadn't seen her dad since sometime last week, and that was only for a few minutes. Losing count of how many days it had been was the norm, not that it mattered; there were always days or weeks in between when she would see him, but it was never for long enough. It was like passing a stranger on the street, and that thought alone saddened her to the core.

Coral's dad, Jayden to the rest of the village, only ever left his room for food or the occasional checking of the post, sadly grunting a hello to either Coral or Kruze. After everything that had happened, he'd completely lost himself; all he seemed to do was exist in this house, or more like his room, practically part of the furniture. Coral hesitated but decided against calling out to her dad. It never mattered how much time had passed; whenever she called out to him only to be greeted with open arms of heart-wrenching silence, it always stung. She'd always been so close to him growing up, sharing a bond on favourite music and flavours of ice cream, but now, she didn't even know who he was anymore, other than him being just the man who she used to know and call dad when she saw him. It didn't stop her from loving him just as much, though; she would always be his little girl no matter how much time passed by.

Hesitantly turning back to face her bedroom door, Coral opened it gently and was greeted by a slightly cold breeze attacking her skin, causing goosebumps to appear. Coral didn't remember leaving the window open but was grateful for the fresh air. As she sauntered over to close it and began unwrapping her hoodie from her waist, without warning, she was launched onto her bed by some great force barging into her and pinning her down, knocking the air out of her lungs.

Trying with all her might to focus on the intruder above her through shaky breaths, she gave a heavy sigh, smiled, and whispered, "Go to hell, Dylan, scaring me like that."

His husky laugh came out and made her laugh in unison, hit in the face with the powerful musk of old spice and cigarette smoke. His eyes looked a lot darker than usual, slightly bloodshot, too, but just as mysterious as always. When he leant down and kissed her hard, she could taste tobacco on his tongue. Not the tastiest of combinations, but still tasted good to her, mainly because she was used to it now. He always tasted good to her, like a forbidden fruit, or more precisely, a forbidden cigarette.

"Sorry, babe," he said, still laughing, sitting up and dragging Coral into his lap. "Did you get my text? You never replied?"

Coral gave a small laugh. He was so off his face, which she wasn't surprised at, but it always amazed her how much this boy could take without completely losing control.

"Yeah, I did, but I was a little bit too busy trying to learn English Literature to decide on which flavoured condoms you should buy." Dylan raised an eyebrow and kissed her again. "Anyway, what did you decide on?"

"Cherry. Feeling fruity, babe," he said and kissed her hard, sticking his tongue down her throat again. She could taste the vodka this time, and it almost made her gag. Dylan pushed her down onto the bed and straddled her.

The last seven months with Dylan had been pure bliss for Coral. They met one night at a party, and after one drunken, deep conversation, and a whole lot of drunken fun in bed, they decided they were good for each other. Both coming from broken families, they supported each other the only way they could think of: having a dinner for two consisting of cheap booze, drugs or tobacco, followed up by the delicious dessert of bedroom antics.

However, Kruze hated Dylan. They were once friends, but Kruze joined the force, and Dylan went down the path of illegal acts, so it put up a big wall between them. So, to prevent any angry outbursts between them, Dylan would go through the fence at the back of the house, climb up and make his way through Coral's window, and when leaving, go the same way back. Not once had they been caught, but if ever there was an emergency, Dylan would hide in her wardrobe; it was empty enough for him to fit.

Dylan leaned over the edge of Coral's bed and grabbed the bottle of vodka from underneath. He unscrewed the top and poured some into Coral's mouth, spilling some over her chest.

"Oops, would you like something to clean that up with?" Dylan asked, mischief glistening in his eyes. Coral bit her lip and slowly pushed his head downwards, feeling his warm breath against her skin. *How can I say no?* Coral thought.

2

The sound of the doorbell rattled through Coral's head at the same time as it wound its way through her ears as if she'd just been thrashed over the head with something very dense. *How much did I even drink last night?* she thought to herself. Lazily looking to her right, she breathed a slight sigh of both relief and disappointment. No sign of Dylan. Even though she knew they couldn't risk getting caught, she always wished at least once she'd wake up to him giving her morning kisses like other girls did.

Rolling out of bed, holding her head from the instant migraine that had just triggered, she looked at her childlike toadstool clock on the wall and frowned.

Nine o'clock in the morning.

"Who the *hell* has woke me up at this time? I get to sleep in twice a week, and someone decides to deprive me of this simple luxury," Coral groaned under her breath while rolling over and covering her head with her pillow.

The doorbell rang again. Coral groaned even louder and swore under her breath, slowly rolling out of bed, dragging her nightshirt over her head and padding across her bedroom floor. She tottered down the stairs, ready to give whoever was on the other side of the door an earful. Normally Coral would stay in bed past midday on a weekend, and even that was early for her. She enjoyed her sleep as much as a cat did. Some days, she wished the sleep would take her permanently, but it never happened; clearly, someone above had other plans for her.

When Coral opened the front door, she was surprised to see Benji. Tall, muscular, police uniform as pristine and tight as ever, showing off his athletic physique underneath. Coral stood up straighter and opened her eyes fully. She turned her head back towards the hallway and shouted, "Kruze, it's for you," unaware of Kruze's whereabouts in the house, if he was even home at all. She hadn't been awake at this time for so many years on a weekend that she wasn't even aware of his Saturday morning routine.

Benji put a gentle hand on Coral's shoulder, making her turn back around with a small smile playing on her lips. "I've actually come to see you, Coral. Can I come in? I promise I won't take up too much of your time." Coral stepped to the side to let him in, a surprised look on her face, as Kruze reached the front door.

"Benji? What're you doing here?" Kruze asked, standing up a little bit straighter with a steaming mug of coffee in his hand. He was obviously trying to show he could still be ready for a hard day's work and be serious, even when wearing his Star Wars dressing gown.

"He needs to talk to me," Coral said in a sing-song voice, twirling her hair between her fingers. She always liked acting coy around Benji. She knew he liked it, even if he did keep a straight face when she did it.

"You can join us if you want," Benji said to Kruze. He clearly knew time alone with Coral wouldn't end well. She rolled her eyes and headed for the dining room, Benji following behind while Kruze headed for the kitchen to make his colleague a drink.

Once in the dining room, they sat down at the table, facing each other. Benji clasped his hands together in a tight grip on the dining room table, his knuckles turning so white she thought the bone would split through within seconds. Coral leant forward, crossing her arms over each other, smiling in his direction.

There was a party a while ago, one where Benji had made a move on Coral, not realising she was Kruze's little sister. Nothing major happened, but it was enough for Coral to use as blackmail against Benji. She raised her leg under the table and gently rubbed her foot up his leg. She never felt guilty towards Dylan when she did these small 'acts of kindness' towards other guys because she knew Dylan most likely did the same behind her back with other girls. However, they were both too numb to care about silly things; they let normal humans be affected by things like that, those who could actually feel emotions other than wanting to be non-existent to the universe.

"Coral, *don't*," he said sternly, moving his leg away from hers. Coral pouted at him in response.

"So, what have I done? Have I been a bad girl?" Coral asked with a spark in her eyes, the smirk on her face growing.

"Coral, I said *don't*. This is a serious matter, so stop *this* immediately," Benji said, authority in his voice, gesturing towards her flirtatious actions and words. One word sprung to Coral's mind: *attractive*.

"Stop what?" Kruze questioned, entering the room and putting a steaming hot mug down in front of Benji. Coral smirked up at him.

"Nothing, let's just get down to business, shall we," he said, taking a sip from his mug, nodding at Kruze as a thanks for the drink and distraction. "So, Coral, you're an artist, right?"

"Yes. It's nice that you're taking an interest in my passions," she said, continuing to lean forward.

"Spray paint much?" Benji asked, raising an eyebrow.

Coral sat back at this, her eyebrows knitting together to portray confusion across her face. *Spray paint?* she pondered.

"I usually stick to my palette and a brush. Why?"

Benji reached into his pocket and took out his phone. Scrolling through pictures, he showed her one in particular that he was referring to. It was a brick wall with black graffiti spelling out 'Coral is found under the water'; the word 'Coral' was sprayed in pink.

Graffiti, Coral noted, *how basic.*

"Now, let's talk like adults. I'd rather you just admitted this was you rather than me having to press you to tell me the truth and get us all tangled up in a mess that can be hugely avoided. You've committed slight offences before; I'm not bringing those up."

Coral looked at him dumbfounded; graffiti wasn't her thing.

Benji continued, "This was taken around the back of the bookshop in the village."

Coral continued to stare at him, not quite sure where this conversation was going.

"Graffiti is an offence that you can be fined for, Coral. Did you know that?"

Coral sat staring at him for what felt like minutes going by rather than seconds, completely oblivious to his words. She wanted to leave her mark on the world, but why would she pick somewhere so obvious or something, in her view, so un-creative? Offence was well and truly taken, but she tried to keep her cool; she couldn't let mister authority take pride in calling her out and making her look stupid, especially in front of Kruze.

"You think *I* did that? I don't know whether to be offended or *extremely* offended. It's hardly an original piece; it's just scruffy amateur graffiti. I'm way above that when it comes to art," Coral said, leaning her head to one side.

"Why are you being so relaxed about this? It's not a joke," Benji questioned. People always did this, talking to her like she was still 13; it was one of the reasons she got pissed off way too easily.

"Because I didn't do it, *that's* why I'm so relaxed," she said, her voice wobbling slightly, the heat in her beginning to build up.

Benji leaned forward. "Look, Coral, if this is some cry for help, then I can offer help to you. Once the fine is paid for, we could arrange for you to see a counsellor or someone professional if you're feeling troubled about what happened still—"

Coral sat forward abruptly, digging her nails into the wooden table. "What did you just say to me?" she spat out at him. Calm and collected time was over; she was in full-on rage mode now, the fire fully lit and blazing out of control inside her like an extreme version of a bonfire. No extinguisher could put this out; it would take a whole firefighter team, and even then, that was at a push.

Kruze moved his chair back slowly and gently so that he didn't alarm her. "Coral, calm down—"

"Calm down! CALM DOWN? Did you *hear* what he just said to me?" she shouted, frantically looking at her brother. She turned her gaze towards the other police officer in front of her with a raw animal look on her face, snarling. "Say it again, Benji," Coral said, gritting her teeth together, "I *dare* you."

Benji stood his ground despite the anger burning through Coral and radiating like wildfire, which was more than apparent right at this moment. He had hit a nerve with her but needed to keep professional, even if it would more than likely make Coral lash out even more than she was already.

"If you need help with your grieving, then I can support you in getting the help you need. I don't want to find that I ignore the graffiti and that you—"

"That I *what*, Benji?" Coral abruptly stood up, knocking her chair backwards and over onto the laminate. "That I'll *drown* myself? Is that what you think I'm going to do? End my life?"

Benji swallowed so loudly that Coral heard him from across the table; the nerves in him had clearly set in. "I didn't mean to cause offence, Coral. I just think you—"

"Get out before I *punch* you," she growled, a fierce lioness ready to attack her prey, just waiting for the right moment.

"Coral, you can't threaten a police officer like that," Kruze said with a slight sternness to his voice, as if he was trying to warn her as he walked around the table to get to her.

"*Don't* come near me, Kruze," she said, pointing at him. "He just *blatantly* said that I wanted to kill myself. If I was that desperate to kill myself, I would've already done it, Benji. I'd do it without leaving clues. I'd do it *so* quietly," she said, pointing a finger at Benji this time, her voice lowering to not much louder than a whisper, tears burning in her eyes, tempting themselves to spill over any second, but she wouldn't let them. She wouldn't give anyone the satisfaction.

Leaning forward over the table, she tried her best to compose herself while Benji remained where he was, all colour drained from his face. He clearly couldn't handle the truth coming from her lips. "No one would ever find me, Benji, not even *you*. I'd do it so discreetly that no one would notice I was gone for weeks, even months. Everyone would think I'd run away from home, made my great escape with the money in my piggy bank. When in reality, a quick death far from here in the middle of nowhere would be the most likely fate for me."

Coral looked down at the chair she had knocked over. She really hoped she'd scared him. Standing up straight, her gaze not once leaving his, she pushed her shoulders back and focused herself on the situation at hand. "Now, get out of this house. And that's an order, *sir*," she said, at first walking out of the dining room but then running quickly up the stairs, falling into her bedroom, slamming the door right behind her.

Now she was alone, she could let the tears spill out from her eyes and soak her cheeks. She threw herself onto the bed and buried her face into her pillow, silently screaming, sobbing painfully from what had just happened. The pain grew and grew within her, eating away at every organ she had, ripping into her bloodstream, her body aching and pulsing in response. It had been a while since she had felt like this, or at least allowed herself to feel this much pain all at once. The body-shattering pain that tore through her was too much to bear, the reasoning behind it never getting any easier to understand or process.

The loss of her mum.

She had been 13 when the tragedy had happened. She'd been at school when her Aunt Eva came to pick her up halfway through her last lesson of the day. Coral had been extremely nervous on her way to her aunt's car, and seeing her brother sat in the car already, looking just as confused as her, made the whole thing even worse. The drive back home was excruciating, and once they'd gotten home and walked inside, they both felt very weird and strange; something hadn't been right, you could sense that from the second of stepping over the threshold.

Her dad sat in the armchair in the living room, head bowed. A few glasses had been smashed and liquid spilt on the coffee table, which scared Coral. Their home, at that time, had been such a warm and happy place to live in; nothing like *this*. Within a few minutes, Kruze and Coral had been told by their Aunt Eva that their mum had been found in the lake, not far from the water's edge. The police had called it suicide.

The reasoning behind that was the simple facts: her mum's wrists were slit, she was face down in the water, the knife nearby with only her DNA on, and she'd bled out into the lake, turning the beautiful crystal blue water to a murky colour. Tainted; both the water and Coral's thirteen-year-old heart.

Kruze chose to turn the pain he felt into positive energy by joining the force and therefore bringing justice to those who deserved it, but it took a while for him to get that way. He suffered mentally as much as they all had, scarring them for life in a way that would take years to fix, even in the slightest amounts. He couldn't help his mum, so instead he would try to help as many other people as he could for the rest of his life. Even if it wouldn't be enough to take away the initial loss, it helped distract him at least.

On the other hand, Coral had disintegrated inside. The happy-go-lucky teenage girl who took the world in her stride and always smiled turned to dust, and in its place, a pained girl who abused her body with alcohol she snuck from the house and packets of cigarettes that burnt out her lungs which she bought from Alawa. He was one of Iris's cousins, a boy a few years older than her who got his income from students in desperate need of a smoke to help distract them from reality.

Iris tried her best to keep her on the straight and narrow when the tragedy had hit, but found the only way to support Coral was to sit in the woods and watch as a young and broken Coral screamed at the top of her lungs till she felt too tired to go on. But it was never a permanent relief, no matter how many years had passed by.

By the age of 16, Coral was a completely different girl. Her grades had slipped massively, and her drinking and smoking habits became increasingly worse by resorting to more daily than weekly antics; she wanted more ways to abuse her body, more ways to numb the pain and distract herself. Without a doubt, she refused to take a blade to her wrists, though; no way would she repeat her family history. So one day, when she was in the supermarket with Iris, she saw her calling on a shelf and grabbed the box, not caring how much it would cost or what others would think.

"Are you sure about this, Coral?" Iris had asked her with a hint of sternness in her voice. But Coral had already made up her mind and thrust the coral-pink hair dye at her best friend, and by the night-time, her hair was transformed. Kruze had gone mental when she eventually came home, her dad took one look and went back to his room, and Aunt Eva had the exact same reaction as Kruze but worse. The rage in her eyes was hard to miss.

"You'll *never* get into sixth form looking like *that*," she'd said, pointing a finger at her angrily. "They'll expel you, and then where will you go? You'll be another let-down to this family. You can get that fixed immediately." That's when Coral had shown Aunt Eva her middle finger and walked back out of the house, through the fence at the back and sat in the small patch of woodland on her own, drinking her Jack Daniels and smoking as many cigarettes as her sixteen-year-old lungs could take.

After an hour had passed, she heard her aunt's car ignition start and the squeal of the tyres on the street. Within moments of hearing that sound, Kruze came out and sat with her, taking a cigarette and lighting it up. They'd just sat in silence, smoking and passing the bottle between them.

"I know it's hard, Coral. *So* fucking hard," he'd said to her, taking a big chug on the bottle, tears streaming down his face. "But I *promise* you, I *won't* leave your side. I'll *never* leave your side, and neither will Dad. We're all finding our ways to cope, and I promise we can and will get through this." That night, Coral spent the remaining hours before sunrise searching the internet for discreet ways to take her own life, but she came up with nothing as sleep finally engulfed her.

Now, five years later, she still felt as empty and desperate to leave the world as she did that first disastrous day, if not more. The pain may seem to fade when she was distracted, but it always came back just as hard as it did the first time she felt it, never any easier to handle.

It hurt to breathe.

Coral wondered if this was how her dad felt; surely, he must do. All she wanted was to hug her dad, have him hold her tight, stroke her hair and tell her it was okay, to let it all out for as long as she needed to. But he hardly ever came out of his room, even after all this time, and right now, she really wished he would. He worked from home, giving all he could for them, which wasn't much. But right now, she needed him, and he was so vacant in her life. She slipped out of her bedroom and stood at his door. Holding her hand up to knock, she was interrupted when Kruze stormed passed her, grabbing her by the wrist and dragging her back into her room, shutting the door behind them. He sat them both down on her bed and put his arm around her. His reaction was unexpected after what had just happened. *Why is he being so nice when I've just verbally attacked his colleague?* she wondered.

"That was difficult," he said, letting out a deep sigh, his body deflating like a balloon that had seen better days. "It was *really* difficult."

"I'd say I'm sorry, but I'm really not," she said, getting tense again. She may have felt exhausted, but she could easily stand her ground once more if she needed to.

"Don't be sorry," he said, stunning Coral. *He's sticking up for me against one of his own?*

She leant away and looked at him with confusion etched on her face.

He made eye contact with her and cleared his throat. "He had no right to come into this house and accuse you of something, especially the reasoning being so close to home. No right whatsoever," he said, and then he unexpectedly jumped up and kicked at her bedroom wall.

"Kruze," Coral said in a weak voice; all the crying had made her feel beyond exhausted, and she didn't have the energy to stop him. She felt like she needed an oxygen tank and mask to get through this outbreak she'd had.

"He's such a prick. He knows full well how much Mum's death affected this family, and he still said something. I'm going to report him to our chief officer," Kruze said and sat back down, putting his head in his hands. "I'm sorry about that, Coral, really sorry. I just don't like it when people say things like that; making it out like her death is easier for us now that time has passed, because it really isn't. I feel like it was just yesterday that we got taken out of school to go home and find out she'd gone."

Coral felt a sudden urge within herself to wrap her arms around her brother and comfort him, and so she did. What Coral had said to Benji would've hurt Kruze, she knew that. He never knew fully that she still felt like this about their mum's death, or at least he never seemed like he fully acknowledged it, probably trying his best to believe otherwise because he knew there was no immediate cure for her depression. She could tell it had killed him to hear it; after all, he's the big brother, he's supposed to protect her from the evil around her, but sadly, even he couldn't protect her from the evil thoughts floating around in her own head, buried deep in her skin and floating around her bloodstream.

It had hurt her to say it all out loud; saying it in your head is one thing, but saying it out loud where people can hear you, that's something else completely; purely terrifying. It makes it somewhat more real, and then the judgement kicks in and the weird looks and everything else that follows suit. She'd experienced that for the last five years wherever she went, with her coral-coloured hair not helping her to blend in very easily, but why should she spend the rest of her life blending in? She had so many mixed emotions about herself; it was touch and go which one took the lead these days.

Kruze kissed Coral on the head and headed off to get ready for work. Benji was going to feel the wrath from his chief officer, and Coral couldn't wait to hear all about it.

* * * *

The morning and afternoon flew by as Coral threw more and more paint at the everlasting canvas that had been sat on her easel for months. Every now and then, she would find herself sitting on her windowsill watching the clouds roll across the stunning blue sky, smoking a few cigarettes while listening to her music. Coral's phone buzzed, interrupting her from her thoughts. Feeling a lot more relaxed than she had in the morning, she sauntered over to it, pressing the home button to see which darling human had messaged her. It was from Iris.

Reminder: Engagement party tonight. Get to mine for pre-drinks. Wear something hot xox

Coral felt a sudden spark of happiness ignite within her, the events from earlier put behind her for now.

Something she loved most was going to parties, especially those at the lake, where she could drink as much free alcohol as possible and party with her best friend. No one cared, everyone let go of all their worries and just let the environment around them take them to a different level of happiness and joy. She was the life and soul most times, which secured that she always got an invite to the many parties that went on around where she lived, despite her depressive state away from the outside world. As if the message had ignited her, she felt her posture straighten and a spring suddenly in her step as she walked over to her wardrobe and opened it up, excitement flooding throughout her body, all sadness put at bay for the time being. All she saw was black, black and even more black clothes. She dragged out her fitted boob tube dress, which she got as a present for her latest birthday, and decided on that. *Sexy and short,* she thought, *perfect outfit to wear with my leather biker boots.*

Coral got a refreshing cold shower, getting rid of any paint that had made its way onto her skin, and once she'd finished, she wrapped herself up in her crisp white towel and sauntered back through to her bedroom, heading over to her battered dressing table. She gently applied the broken rose gold eye shadow palette to her eyes and stroked the black eyeliner across her lids, followed by the booming mascara to add to the look and enhance the largeness of her eyes even more. *I definitely get my eyes from Mum*, she thought and smiled to herself.

While looking for her favourite lipstick in one of the drawers, she came across a charm from a charm bracelet; a small cactus. Not just anyone's charm bracelet, though, her mum's, one that she never took off when she was alive. However, when the police found her body, she wasn't wearing it, and the police never found it. They assumed it had succumbed to the depths of the lake, so they dismissed it due to the death being suicide, finding it wouldn't have been important to the investigation. However, thirteen-year-old Coral thought very differently to the police and couldn't understand this and therefore was upset at the thought of her mum's bracelet going missing when it was so special to her. So, she took it upon herself and went down to the lake days later, once the investigation had closed, to see if she could find it. But all she found after hours of searching was the cactus charm her dad had got her mum after they'd been on a family holiday to California.

Coral's dad had given her mum the charm bracelet as a gift when they first got together, and every time they went somewhere together, or if anything special happened in their lives that was especially meaningful, he would always get her a charm to add to the bracelet. Coral had always loved to look at the charm bracelet and hear her mum explain to her all the stories behind each charm. So, once she found the cactus, she kept it in the back of her drawer in her dressing table, always there to remind her of a good memory she had with her family when life wasn't so painful.

Holding the cactus in the palm of her hand, she squeezed it and gave a small smile, a single tear running down her face. She quickly dabbed at it with a tissue, making sure it hadn't ruined her makeup, and put the cactus charm back into the drawer, snatching up the lipstick and quickly applying it, smacking her lips together and smiling back at her reflection.

"I'll party for both of us, Mum."

3

Looking up at the quaint stone-built house Iris lived in, Coral felt a sharp pain in her chest. Inside the house there was a happy family, which was only filled with positivity and love, and not so many ghosts haunting and hurting. This is why Coral loved spending time here; she felt more like she was part of a family here than she did in her own home.

She walked up to the door and knocked three times, only to be greeted by a beaming bodacious Luciana, Iris's mum. "Ah, Coral, you beautiful lady, come inside. You'll catch a cold dressed like that," she said in her Latina accent.

Luciana and her late husband, Matías, moved from Chile to England back in the eighties before they had Iris, preferring the English culture to their own and less of the dictatorship and other government changes in Chile. They particularly loved the look of the Lake District, and they were lucky enough to set up home there. They only lived a short walking distance from Coral's home, which was very convenient for her if she ever needed a shot of normality back into her system.

"Luciana, it's literally 20 degrees outside. I've got more chance of catching a sunburn than a cold," Coral said, smiling as she'd been engulfed in a hug. Luciana's hugs were as close to feeling like her mum's as she could get any more, so she always closed her eyes and imagined they were really hers.

"You better have sun cream on with that pearlescent skin of yours, then," she said, giving Coral a knowing look. She turned and walked into the hallway, shouting, "Carena, Coral is here." Coral twitched at the use of Iris's birth name. She'd always referred to her as Iris, so hearing her called anything other than that just sounded foreign to her.

As Coral followed behind Luciana through the hallway and into the open-plan kitchen-diner and living room, she saw Iris standing in the kitchen making cocktails to pre-drink with, obviously using her fancy cocktail glasses. Coral was more of a 'drink straight out of the bottle' kind of girl, but she appreciated it when Iris made the effort for them both, taking the edge off of slumming it in the woods in a hoodie, necking on a bottle of something strong, which was Coral's usual go-to. Not very classy, but that summed up Coral.

Iris walked over to the ice dispenser, her fluffy slippers slapping on the stylish marble floor, and pressed a glass against the lever, but all they heard was a loud clunk.

"Damn, all out. Mum, come help me get the ice from the freezer round the back, please," she said, sliding through a side door with her mum trailing behind. Coral stood awkwardly peering into the glasses at the contents.

"Looking forward to your evening by the lake, Coral?" Aaron asked her. She was completely unaware of him sitting there in his usual armchair, and so she flinched at the unexpected voice.

Aaron was Luciana's recent fiancé. He'd asked her only four months ago, and she was dubious of saying yes to another man, especially with only having been with Aaron for three and a half years. But since it had been 10 years since Matías passed away, she felt it was time to accept love again, the love she'd missed out on for so many years.

Matías, as much as Coral could remember, was one of the loveliest people she'd known. He'd always made time for his family, worked hard to provide for them, and made the best fajitas she'd ever tasted. She was too young to remember his loss on a great emotional level but always stood by Iris as much as she could to support her. A loss is a loss no matter how long ago; she felt that on a personal level.

"Yeah, the parties down at the lake are always good, especially this time of year," Coral said, pulling her dress down at the hem. She hadn't realised how much it had ridden up while walking to Iris's house.

"So I've heard," he said with a grin. "Have you got your drinks at the ready, or do you need a lift to the shop?"

"Got it at the ready," she said, moving her carrier bag ever so slightly, making the bottles and cans inside it gently clink together.

Aaron smiled in response. "Sounds like a promising night then," he said, turning back to his newspaper. After a few seconds had passed, he said out loud, "You don't half look like your mother." With that, he looked back up at Coral and then at the photos on the wall, referring to a picture that was gathered among all of Luciana's family photos, and this photo was very special to Iris.

It was a photo of Iris and Kruze baking a cake, or more like attempting to and failing. There was flour and eggs everywhere, and they were laughing harder than ever before. Coral's mum was in the picture, also laughing at the burnt cake that she'd just taken out of the oven to show them. They were very young at the time but were trying to be independent. Coral smiled at the picture and gave a small laugh in response, saying, "Well, I should hope so; I'd be very worried if not."

Before any more could be said, Iris and Luciana walked back into the kitchen-diner.

"I don't know why you needed me to find the ice, it was right in front of your eyes, girl. Try opening them in future," Luciana said, taking her glass of wine from the worktop and taking a large sip.

"Come here, my *ángel hermoso*," Aaron said, patting his lap and folding away his newspaper. Luciana smiled warmly and climbed into the armchair with Aaron, snuggling up to him. This sort of affection didn't bother Iris, the proof showing as she continued to make the cocktails aimlessly. Coral rolled her eyes as Iris started chopping fruit carefully.

"You're in the wrong business. You're wasted as a business lady with cocktail-making skills like these." She smirked, taking her place at the kitchen island.

"Wasted? Try telling that to my vehicle outside. The business lady you're talking to right *now* is who put that in the driveway," she said, smiling to herself. Iris had done brilliantly with what she had achieved since school, flying high with her career in business and smashing all of the courses and obstacles they put in her way. If only Coral could feel as motivated about school and life as her friend did. "I've got a meeting with the headquarters of a major skincare product next week, so I've got to be at the top of my game for it and pitch at the highest level to them. I can't be losing out on money for the company, or my purse for that matter."

Placing the chopped-up fruit into the cocktails, she lifted them up, passing one to Coral. "Perfect! Are you ready to have a bit of class before we move ourselves onto the main event?"

"You bet I am," Coral responded, eyes glistening at the drink in front of her, clinking glasses with Iris. "Let the drinking commence!"

* * * *

Bounding up the stairs, being careful not to spill their drinks, they went up to Iris's bedroom so she could get ready, so Coral took this opportunity to be the DJ while she got changed. The more she drank her pre-drink cocktail, the quicker she could feel the effects of the alcohol kicking in, and so she smiled to herself, kicking off her boots and standing on Iris's bed. Coral swayed her hips and started to sing as loud as she could.

Iris came out of her en suite, all done up to the nines, walking in as if she was on the catwalk. "How do I look?" she asked dramatically, doing a twirl and posing.

Coral smirked and sank down onto the bed. "I swear you only own one dress. I can't remember a party we went to where you didn't wear your red dress."

Iris beamed at her. "It's my favourite, and it always will be. Also, you *didn't* answer my question?"

"Looks to me like some guy's jaws are going to be on the floor from looking at you, and the girls are going to be very jealous. When's Onida picking us up?" Coral asked, putting down her empty cocktail glass and swapping it for taking a big sip from her bottle of mixed cocktail. Before she stepped out of her house, she added many alcoholic drinks from her room into an empty water bottle, along with as many loose bottles and cans as she could find. She called it the 'Death Wish Blend'. The reason why was in the title of the name and how you felt the next morning after consuming it.

"He text me not long ago, so he should be here soon."

* * * *

Once Iris and Coral had finished drinking and dancing around Iris's bedroom, they made their way down the stairs and headed for the front door, sliding their footwear on.

"Have fun, girls, and most importantly, stay safe and watch your drinks," Luciana shouted to them, always showing concern for them no matter what age they were.

"Promise we will," they both said in unison and headed out of the front door, trailing their alcohol behind them in a big reusable carrier bag, holding a handle each.

"Come on, girls, I haven't got all night. I've got a date that I need to get to," Onida yelled from the open window of his SUV. Coral always felt like she was walking up to a limo with how big it was, but it needed to be to fit all of Iris's cousins in. Iris always felt lucky that she was an only child, whereas her cousin Onida didn't fall that lucky, and he ended up with twin brothers Akule and Alawa, then Nitis was born, and lastly, Lokni. Their mum and dad came over from Chile at the same time as Luciana and Matías, only living a twenty-minute drive away, so they always stayed close growing up; they were more like her brothers than her cousins.

"I love that you still call it a date even though you've been with Rosa for two years," Iris said, climbing into the back of the car with Coral in pursuit.

"Date nights last all the way through no matter how long you're with them, Carena; maybe one day you'll experience that yourself," Onida retorted.

Once they'd clambered into the back of the SUV and fastened themselves in, Akule yelled, "Time to go party, my dudes," and the music suddenly blasted louder from the speakers, the bass vibrating through the vehicle as they began their journey to the lake. Two cans were passed to the back for Coral and Iris to drink. *The more the merrier*, Coral thought, sitting back and basking in the moment.

****

As soon as the road to the lake was in sight, Coral's heart leapt. The happiness she got from just seeing the lake was enough to adjust her lips into the biggest grin. Onida looked in the rear-view mirror and caught a glimpse of the happiness lighting up Coral's face. "Nearly there now, Coral; brace yourself," he said as he pushed his foot down ever so slightly on the accelerator, but it was enough to jump the SUV forwards to a greater speed, and everyone made sounds of pure excitement and delight. It wasn't just an escape from reality for Coral; it was an escape for everyone.

Once they got there, they all climbed out of the SUV, grabbing their bags of drinks and snacks from the boot.

"Thanks for the lift, Onida. I'll drop you a text later on," Iris said, leaning on the rolled-down window of the car door on the driver's side.

"You're welcome, but make sure you all make it out alive. I don't want any trips being made to the hospital tonight," he said, no hint of amusement on his face at all.

"I'll do my best. Oh, and enjoy your *date night.*" Iris smirked, moving away from the car just in time so she was out of reach from Onida's hand, which was ready to clip her around the head. She laughed as he drove away, waving enthusiastically with one of her long slender arms.

Coral was busy opening up another can when Nitis came over to her. "Slow down, buddy. You'll run out of alcohol before you know it," he said, chuckling to himself. Nitis had something about him, and Coral couldn't explain what it was. It was like an aura, something she'd never experienced before, not even with Dylan. She was drawn to him in ways she couldn't put into words, whether it was because of his constant windswept hair, his big brown eyes, or his slim yet well-built tanned body; it all just made her want him more and more each time she saw him, but of course, she kept those thoughts to herself.

She laughed in response. "Not entirely, because once *my* alcohol is gone, I can start on the *free* alcohol."

He smiled at her in a way that caused unexplainable feelings inside. "Quite smart, aren't you, Coral?"

"Oh, you don't know the half of it, *buddy*," she said, winking at him and smirking, enjoying the little moment they were having.

"Will you two love birds shut up and carry some bags; we've got a party to get to," Akule said, nudging his bag into Nitis's leg and walking down the dirt track leading to the party. Nitis looked down, smiling and then looked back up at Coral.

"After you, m'lady," he said, winking back at her. Coral smiled and started to follow the others down the dirt track.

There were paths that led off to different parts of the surroundings of the lake, and they made their way down the one that led to a small, wooded picnic area. As they got closer to the party destination, they could see the twinkling fairy lights of all colours ahead of them, balloons tied to trees, and the aroma of barbeque food cooking away. A big white paper sign with purple cursive writing on read 'Engagement Party for Brianna and Mason: Time to get merry before married!'

"Looks like the right place," Iris said, smiling triumphantly that she had found it so well in what was left of the light from the setting sun.

"Yeah, because there's plenty of other engagement parties we could've ended up crashing accidentally around here," Alawa said in his serious tone, adjusting his long hair so it fell over one shoulder.

"Piss off, Alawa, and let's have less of the sarcasm for at least one night, please," Iris said as the guys laughed in unison.

"Hey, you never know; I hear the lake is the perfect place for an engagement party, especially this night in particular. There could be loads of potential engagements scattered around the area," Lokni said jokily, making his way past the group to put his bag down on the nearest pop-up table.

"And you'd know this *how*?" Iris asked pointedly, crossing her arms over her chest, a look on her face as if to humour him.

"Iris, tonight is a very special night; it's the night we make Lokni a *man*," Akule said, and Lokni beamed in response.

"Breaking news: Lokni speaks to a girl for the first time and doesn't mess it up," Nitis said in a similar voice to a news broadcaster, using a bottle as a pretend microphone. The guys laughed again in unison. Coral smirked slightly, trying her hardest not to laugh.

"I've got loads of girls lined up to talk to me actually. At least my only option for pleasure isn't just a blow-up doll like it is for *you* lot," Lokni said, crossing his arms over his chest. Coral and Iris doubled over laughing, but Alawa quickly pushed Iris over into a bush, making her scream out and swear.

Akule turned to Lokni and said, pointing in his face, "Any more of *that* language, dude, and you'll be getting sent back home quicker than you can blink, and I mean the home overseas."

Lokni grinned, knowing full well that he had hit a nerve with his brother. Out of all of the brothers, Coral noticed, Lokni was the palest of them all, which wasn't by much as they all had olive skin, and his hair was more mousy brown, unlike his brothers, who had hair as dark as nearly being on the verge of black in colour. If she didn't know them personally, she would've said he was definitely not from the same dad as the rest of them, but sometimes genes transfer differently with children.

He darted off into the party, trailing behind Iris, who had stormed off after clambering out of the bush, swatting leaves and insects off her dress and picking them out of her hair. She handed her present over to the newly engaged couple, beaming and regaining her composure. Everyone followed ahead, looking around at the small pop-up tables holding heavy amounts of alcohol, snacks, and one hell of a decorative cake.

Coral said aloud, "That's one hell of an impressive cake. I've never seen anything quite like it; it's so beautiful."

"It sure is," Nitis said, looking down at Coral and smiling. She looked up at him and smiled back, then snapped out of her trance and remembered where she was.

"Right, time for a drink. Fancy doing a few shots?" she asked, daring him with her eyes and a wicked smile.

"A few isn't in my vocabulary," he said, once again winking at her, as they sauntered off to the nearest alcohol-packed table.

* * * *

The party was just what Coral needed; dancing away with her friends, drinking whatever she wanted when she wanted, and just letting go. She walked over to the newly engaged couple with Iris so she could be introduced.

"Mason, Brianna, this is Coral, my plus one," she said, grinning. They both smiled at her, and Mason gave her a thoughtful look.

"Aren't you Kruze's little sister?" he asked, putting his arm around Brianna while having a drink out of his beer bottle.

"If I got a pound for every time I heard that, I'd be *beyond* minted by now," Coral replied, smiling and holding her hand up, rubbing her thumb against her index finger and middle finger.

"Yeah, he's a good one, that lad, done my family a lot of good over the years round by our neck of the woods. You should be proud of him," Mason said, sipping from his beer bottle again. Brianna beamed at him.

"Check you out, complimenting people," she said to him, then turned to Coral and Iris and said, "I think this engagement has changed him."

"Couldn't harm, could it?" Iris said, laughing, clinking glasses with Brianna.

* * * *

Later on into the night, Coral walked over to Alawa and held out a five-pound note. He opened his jacket pocket and passed her a packet of cigarettes but pushed away the hand holding the money. Before she could argue, he said, "That one's on the house, Coral. Just light up and enjoy, free of charge."

She lit one up off of his current cigarette and sucked hard on it, letting her lungs become polluted. As she breathed out, both herself and Alawa couldn't help but laugh at Akule's attempts to win over a picnic table full of girls. Some of them were listening to him and enjoying the attention, some merely finding him entertaining. One of the girls started twirling his hair around her fingers and went in for the kiss, but she was quickly interrupted by Lokni pouring ice down the back of Akule's shirt. The girl held her hand over her mouth, giggling hysterically while Akule hastily got up and set off in a sprint, with a determined look on his face, through the trees, making a beeline for Lokni.

"Get back here, you little shit," left his mouth and echoed around the woods surrounding them. Coral couldn't help but double over laughing and coughing from the smoke, Alawa joining in too.

Alawa said, "Excuse me, I have business to attend to," and made his way over to the table where the girl was still giggling from what had happened to Akule. She turned her attention to him, and after what seemed like seconds, she'd placed her hand on his knee, laughing at something he'd said. He looked at Coral out of the corner of his eye, winked, and proceeded to converse with the pretty girl at the picnic table, which within moments became more kissing than talking. *Perks of being an identical twin,* Coral thought.

* * * *

Slowly raising her head from the picnic table, Coral looked around in utter confusion. The time wasn't what was concerning Coral, but more the fact that it had gone by, and she had no idea how long she'd been sitting alone or how she got to the table in the first place. A blurry figure began drifting its way towards her, and after blinking her eyes a few times, the blur turned into a smiling figure she knew. As she went to stand up, she sat back down with a thump and grabbed her head, feeling a bit worse for wear than she usually did at parties.

Nitis quickly sat down next to her, wrapping one arm over her shoulder and saying words that were inaudible to her. Coral's memory of the previous hours was slowly shifting from her mind and turning into one big blur. She leaned into Nitis and started giggling nervously.

"Are you okay?" he asked, smiling to reassure her, but the concerned look on his face wasn't well disguised.

"Yeah, of course, why wouldn't I be? I'm drunk, so I couldn't be happier if I tried," Coral lied, her vision getting worse by the second, tilting in every angle possible, making her head spin. The environment around her was spinning out of control, and black dots appeared before her making everything look fuzzy, like static on a TV, so she blinked as hard as she could to try and get her vision back to normal.

Nitis lifted up her chin so she was looking at him. "You're beyond drunk, and yet you still look as gorgeous as ever," he said, smiling down at her, his eyes looking sleepy, his face a mixture of black dots.

Coral smiled, not fully aware of her facial expression, but she knew she'd be showing him the cheesiest smile right now, one that even Dylan hadn't witnessed.

"You have a way with words, Nitis," she slurred.

"You have a way with..." he said, but as she was trying to hear the end of the sentence, all she could feel was the warmth of his arms wrapping around her as everything went dark.

4

Coral took a deep breath in her sleep, which caused her to choke on unwanted saliva, and she woke with a sudden start. He was here. She could smell his aftershave coating the room as she smiled and stretched her arms above her head, her body aching more than it usually did after a party, so her arms flopped back down onto the bed. *What on earth happened last night?* she wondered.

"Coral?"

She slowly tried to sit up, only just managing to lean back on one of her elbows, her head spinning and her insides fluttering at the sound of her name on his lips. Not feeling as though she had enough strength within her, she gently sank back down as the sick feeling started to rise up in her throat. He stood up and walked over, smiling at her with such warmth and care. She couldn't remember the last time someone had looked at her that way or even made her feel how she felt at the sight of him.

"What are you doing in my bedroom? Was I *that* drunk?" she asked, raising an eyebrow and smirking.

Nitis smirked back at her. "No, you just passed out, so I rang Onida, and we brought you home. We didn't want to disturb Kruze or your dad, so we found your keys and carried you in through the front door. If anyone had seen us, they'd have thought we'd been kidnapping you and decided to take you back," he said, sniggering and Coral giggled too at the thought of it.

Nitis continued. "I decided to stay and slept on the floor wrapped up in a blanket. I just wanted to make sure you were okay through the night. You really didn't seem well, like, you were completely zoned out last night, and you couldn't even focus your eyes. I've seen you drunk before, but that was a whole new level." He took a step forward and gently sat down on Coral's bed, so close to her, and folded his hand around hers, giving it a gentle squeeze. She liked that. "How're you feeling?" he asked, putting his free hand on her forehead.

Coral squeezed her eyes shut for a few seconds before replying to Nitis. "Rough, like *really* rough. I honestly didn't think I'd drank so much last night, and that's rich coming from me, but I really didn't," Coral said, rubbing her eyes with her free hand and squeezing his hand, which was still wrapped around hers.

"You seemed fine to me for the majority of the night. You started acting strange not long after Dylan had finished talking to you. You seemed really out of it real quick, and not long after that you passed out while we were sat talking," Nitis said, looking concerned now, his big brown eyes showing such kindness. Dylan wasn't his favourite person in the world, or many people's for that matter, but he respected Coral and her choices. Well, to some extent, he knew Dylan was one of her many coping mechanisms.

Coral's eyebrows knitted together. "Dylan was there? Why was he there?" she asked, reaching over for her phone to find there were no texts or calls from him. *Nice to know he cares*, she thought.

"No idea, but you guys were talking, walked away out of sight, and then you came back after a while, and I found you sat at the picnic table on your own. As

I explained, you were completely out of it. Strange how it happened so quickly after that," Nitis said, shifting uncomfortably and looking away. She knew exactly what he was thinking; he just didn't want to offend her by saying it out loud.

"He wouldn't have..." Coral didn't finish her sentence after looking at Nitis. His eyes bored into her, and his face had a questioning look as if he was about to say something along the lines of *you honestly believe he wouldn't spike your drink and take advantage of you?*

He smiled at her and stroked her head gently, which was so soothing to Coral that she leant into his hand, closing her eyes. "I'm just glad you're okay now."

Nitis's phone made a tinkling noise from across the room, so he slowly got up, crossed the room, and crouched down to where his phone was on the carpet. As he got back up, he pocketed his phone and walked over to sit by Coral again. He opened his mouth to speak but thought better of whatever he wanted to say.

"What is it?" she asked, watching as he tried his best to suppress the laugh that was rising up through his throat, so he started coughing, but it didn't work. "Nitis, tell me what's so funny."

"Well," he started, running one hand through his mane, "*you* might not find it so funny, but the queen is arriving soon, or should I say, the colonel of my family."

Coral put her hands up to her head, another sudden rush of feeling woozy and sick. *What on earth happened to me last night?* she wondered.

"Why is Iris on her way?" she mumbled like a child who'd just been told off or knew full well she was in for a blasting. Nitis started laughing.

"You know why she's coming here," he said, smirking the entire time. "She only cares about you, Coral."

"There's caring, and then there's acting like we're in the army and she's my sergeant. Do I have time to hide?" she asked, searching her eyes around the room for the perfect place to pretend she didn't exist, but just as the thoughts started to race around her mind, she heard a knock at the front door and Kruze's feet pounding down the stairs.

Coral heard her brother and Iris greet each other, asking how they'd both been, giving light-hearted little amounts of detailed answers to one another. Once again, she heard feet pounding on the stairs, but this time, not as heavy-footed. Coral counted out the seconds, one, two, three, and her bedroom door swung open. Coral quickly stuffed her head underneath her pillow and pulled the duvet up over her as high as she could. She loved Iris with all of her heart, but the lectures she could do without, especially when she felt like death warmed up.

"Coral, you can't just bury yourself under your covers and hide," Iris said, sitting on the right-hand side of the bed at the end. "You know I respect you and support you, but he took one step too far this time."

Coral pulled the pillow tighter over her head. *Maybe*, she thought, *if I hold it down hard enough, I'll lose consciousness and can avoid this situation altogether.* She could hear mumbling as Nitis and Iris spoke to each other quietly. Without warning, the pillow over her head was pulled from her grasp and blaring sunlight plastered across her face as Nitis pulled back the curtains, stinging her eyes.

"You're trying to kill me," Coral murmured, pulling the duvet over her head but not holding tight enough as Iris leaped up and pulled it from the bottom of the bed and onto the floor. Coral gasped; despite the fact it was summertime, her home always remained cold inside, ironically, and so as the cold air of her room stabbed at her skin, causing goosebumps to creep up her arms and legs, she sat up and scowled at Iris, pointing a finger at her best friend, screwing her eyes shut in response to the eye-burning brightness of the room.

"I could've been naked under that duvet for all you knew." She looked down at herself, unaware of what she was wearing; her strapless black dress still clung to her body. She clocked eyes with Nitis. "You didn't undress me when you brought me home. That's really gentleman-like of you."

He gave her a bashful smile, running one hand through his hair again. *Wow*, she thought, *this boy doesn't half look good doing the most effortless things*. "It's a good job you didn't try to undress me, to be honest. The fact I was unconscious wouldn't have been much help for the boner you'd have got from seeing me dress-less, would it?" she said, picking the nail varnish off her fingers, letting it fall onto her bedsheet. Nitis chuckled to himself while Iris rolled her eyes.

"I didn't need to hear that," she said, no louder than a whisper, her hand against her forehead showing how quickly she was losing her patience with Coral. "Now," she said, regaining composure, smoothing her hands over her velvet grey two-piece tracksuit, "go wash your face, brush your teeth, and get changed. We're going out for some fresh air."

Coral's smug look was quickly wiped off her face at the revelation of having to leave the house. This was Iris's usual routine when Coral had 'overdone it' at a party; however, she was never prepared for it, usually hoping Iris would forget. But Iris never forgot.

As Coral opened her mouth to speak, Iris held up a hand to stop her and said, "No disagreements; just get ready. We'll wait for you in the truck."

Iris marched out of the room with Nitis trailing behind her, smiling lazily at Coral with his big beautiful brown eyes. *That boy is something else,* she thought.

Once her bedroom door closed behind them, Coral sighed, but she wasn't sure whether it was a sigh of relief at having peace and quiet finally or gratefulness for having Iris and her family in her life. No one could draw her out of her miserable mindset more than Iris could, and as much as there were times that it frustrated her, it only ever lasted seconds and was replaced with thankfulness. She'd always put Coral first no matter what else was happening in her life, and for that, she was beyond lucky; she knew no one else would ever do that for her.

Swinging her legs over the edge of the bed, she carefully placed her feet on the floor and made a move towards her wardrobe, stumbling over and trying her best to grab a pair of denim faded shorts and a white vest top. As she slowly shimmied out of her dress, she flinched from touching her hips. Carefully, as she pulled the rest of the material down her body, she looked in her full-length mirror at herself and let her mouth gape open, shock and confusion etched on her face. *How have I ended up with deep bruising on my hip bones and scratch marks on my thighs?* Coral wondered, *and more to the point, why does it look like fingers have been there?*

* * * *

Succeeding in making herself look more presentable, she carefully made her way down the steps in her cropped jeans, choosing to cover up her legs to avoid the humiliating conversation with Nitis and Iris about why she had the marks on her legs, as she had literally no idea how they'd got there in the first place. As she locked the door behind her and shuffled over to the truck, she opened the truck door and took a steady step forwards and fell into it rather than hopping in as usual. A groan escaped her lips, and Iris looked back at her.

"You're really not okay. I swear if he spiked you last night, I'll kill him," Iris said as Nitis got out and helped Coral into her seat comfortably, strapping her in the best he could in the gentlest way.

"Are you sure you're going to be alright?" he asked her, concern written all over his face. Coral nodded and laid her head back against the headrest but quickly tipped her head back upright, groaning as the pain on her hips pulsed and ached, making her feel very uncomfortable.

"I feel like hell," Coral mumbled, not finding any energy to communicate properly. "Just set off. I've survived worse."

Iris gave her a knowing look in the rear-view mirror. "There's something you're not telling me," she said, raising an eyebrow in anticipation.

"Iris, please just drive. I'm not in the mood," Coral said, leaning her head back once again, twisting her neck in different ways against the headrest, trying her best to get comfortable but failing miserably.

"Oh, I'll drive," Iris said, putting the truck in gear and slowly pulling away from the kerb. "You'll tell me what's wrong in your own time. You always do."

She chose not to mention the bruising on her hips or the scratches on her thighs during the car journey; she didn't want the Secadas lashing out at her or hunting Dylan down, not until she got her say first.

Without a doubt, Dylan was front row of her mind at this moment, but she was trying her best to focus on the fact she was about to devour the mouth-watering food at Iris's and the rest of the Secadas usual Sunday family picnic and that was enough to bring a smile to her face.

The aching in her bones and soreness on her skin was hard to ignore, and so were the thoughts running through her head about Dylan; she was utterly confused about the events from the night before. She *always* remembered the night before, no matter how drunk she'd been… but this time felt different. At least she was looking forward to getting to eat soon, otherwise she'd have been full of rage and anger as to why she was suffering so badly today.

Coral always felt enthused to go along to the Secadas' family picnics; it was one of the only things she got excited about these days. Ever since losing her mum, she was always welcomed as a Secada, despite her difference in skin tone and bright pink hair, but she could pretend they'd adopted her at least; they never treated her any differently.

During the drive, while indie music was making its way through the speakers, Coral tried to really think hard about what could've happened the night before, the thought of it irritating her brain like an itch. Dylan wouldn't have had the balls to drug her, and why would he anyway? It's not like Coral turned him down often or at all; she always caved in. That's one thing he was always good at, getting her right where he wanted her. She loved it and hated it at the same time. He was like marmite to her; some days she loved him, others she couldn't stand him.

Coral was addicted to Dylan, and that was the plain and simple explanation and truth, but she knew very well that addictions weren't good or the answer to a straightforward life. Also, why would he have even been at the party? He could've known Brianna or Mason from school, but still, surely he would've told her he'd be there so she could've crashed at his for the night or had a make-out session behind the trees like they usually would? It had sort of become their tradition; unless it was a house party, they'd roll a dice or flip a coin and pick a room that way. Even if it meant making out in a bath, they weren't fussy.

Dismissing the thoughts whirring around her head, she finally opened her eyes and saw they were almost at the picnicking side of the lake where it was all open space, fields for miles, where families would go on summer days to enjoy food with their loved ones. Luckily it was far away from the part of the lakeside where her mum had been found.

Once the truck stopped, Nitis hopped out and opened Coral's door, helping her out of the truck as delicately as he could. Wrapping his arms around her waist, he slid one of his hands onto her hip to steady her. Coral let out a groan and flinched, forcing shock onto Nitis's face.

"Sorry, did I hurt you?" he blurted out, his cheeks showing a hint of pink. Coral shook her head and smiled.

"No, I'm okay," she said, reaching out to him to help her again. This time, he took her hands, lifting her out of her seat, and then wrapped his arms around her, lifted her up and placed her feet-first onto the ground. Taking in a deep breath of fresh air, she was startled at how much better she was starting to feel, and she knew the weakness throughout her body could surely be overcome with delicious food and good company.

Trudging over to the picnic bench where the rest of the Secadas were, she spotted Onida cooking up some delicious hot dogs and burgers while the twins were throwing a frisbee back and forth to each other. A sense of calm let itself ripple throughout Coral's body, all thoughts of her unexplainable pains pushed aside for later. This family in front of her, all happy and laughing and making the most of their day, was a sight that brought her relaxation and gratefulness, making her feel warm and bubbly inside. Evaporating before her eyes were the negative thoughts she'd possessed since acknowledging the marks on her skin, unknown memories and pain of the night before fluttering away; they were behind her for now; the beautiful world she had grown up in was surrounding her and in full sight, and she couldn't wait to swallow up the deliciousness of the views once again, feel the sun on her skin and breathe in the sweet hot scent of the food her stomach was growling like a bear for.

5

"What a wonderful Wednesday morning it is, class," Miss Clayton started from the front of the classroom. "The sun is shining, the birds are singing, and how convenient is it that I've set you up a project to get on with for the last few weeks of your sixth form experience?" She beamed as the class, in unison, let out a variety of groans, as well as the odd few swear words that were grumbled, luckily out of ear shot of Miss Clayton.

"How is it Wednesday already?" Coral muttered to herself, the last two sixth form days a complete blur. *Why can't sixth form just be one day a week?* she thought.

"You probably slept through Monday and Tuesday," Darcy said, seated next to her with her nose turned up as it always was, as if she'd just sniffed the lack of deodorant Miss Clayton had on. "Either that or you just skived for two days. Isn't that your usual go-to method?"

Coral chose to ignore Darcy's snippy comments and turned her attention back to what was happening in the classroom.

English Literature lessons were usually a dream to Coral, but she knew that projects came with having a project partner, and that never sat well for her. *Not like it matters*, Coral thought to herself, *why should I care that no one ever chooses to work with me on projects and that everyone will make a beeline to every other student in the room so that they obviously don't have to be left with me as a project partner. Who would pick little miss destructive anyway?* No matter how much fun Coral was at parties and other social gatherings, when the alcohol and buzz from the cigarettes weren't present, Coral was little miss doom and gloom at school; it was clearly just in her nature to be that way inclined.

"Go ahead and choose a partner to sit with so we can start discussing the project in hand," Miss Clayton announced to the humid room full of students.

Coral sat back in her chair, crossing her arms over her chest, and proceeded to roll her eyes as she watched Darcy Allerton in her haste to remove herself as fast as she could from the seat beside Coral. It's not like Coral was ever a fan of alphabetical seating arrangements herself. She wished she'd been born with a last name beginning with the letter Z so she could sit as far away from everyone as possible in the back corner rather than up front where she could be constantly watched and judged by every teacher, the 'splash zone' in some teachers cases with their horrendous spitting issues.

Her thoughts were interrupted by the chair next to her being filled as quickly as it was vacated. She daringly looked towards her left to see the cheerful cherub who had taken the seat next to her, hair tied up high on her head and descending in the tightest of ringlets down her back, while her yellow and white floral dress was brighter to look at by the second, a matching bow tied into her hair. Coral would've rubbed her eyes in astonishment if she hadn't plastered them in makeup this morning, trying to hide the everlasting eye bags she had.

"I hope you don't mind, Coral, but I'd *really* love to work with you on this project," Molly Edwards said, beaming at her with her slightly gapped teeth. Coral continued to stare at miss sunshine in complete astonishment. *Surely this is a joke*, she thought. "I feel like we'd make a great team, and what a way to end our time here with a new friendship."

"Do you really think that?" Coral asked, placing her elbows on the table. "And why is it that you think these things, Molly?" She could humour the grinning girl, at least.

"Um... well, you're so creative and headstrong, and I just thought we could make something... really unique with both of our qualities. Plus, I think you're a great person, and I'd love to become firm friends with you. You're like a breath of fresh air to this class in my eyes."

Coral's eyebrows shot up in surprise. No one had ever approached her and described her with words like these since she was a child. No one ever made an effort to get to know her anymore. They already knew everything they needed to know; she was the depressed motherless girl who classed her friends as those that came in bottles and packets. Who'd want to be friends with *that* sort of person?

Coral felt a small spark of joy at the possibility of this being real, but it was quickly extinguished by a feeling of concern and uneasiness at her potential humiliation if the words Molly was speaking weren't full of truth.

"Okay," Coral turned around in her seat, scanning the mass of students in the room, "which one of these set you up?"

"Set me up? No one's set me up, Coral," Molly said, placing a gentle hand on Coral's arm, which caught her off guard and made her flinch. "I did this off my own back; I meant everything I just said." She gave Coral a caring smile, showing she wasn't against her.

Coral was unfamiliar with this way of communication; usually those who interacted with her at school struggled due to conflict in their minds. Will I get picked on for talking to Coral? Will she be a bad influence on me? Can you catch depression like you can catch a cold?

"Right, class, now you're in your pairs, please turn your attention towards the whiteboard, and I will explain to you just what this project is all about." Miss Clayton rose out of her chair, revealing her extremely bulbous body, and as she lifted her arm to point to the white board, Coral noticed the dark patches under her arms on her top and grimaced. *Why would you choose to wear a thick shirt on a hot day?* Coral wondered to herself. Then she imagined how slick and damp her teacher's back would be from the thick shirt, and it was enough to make her retch.

When Miss Clayton noticed no one was listening, she ran a hand through her matted permed hair, twisting it around her finger, clearly anxious about having to interrupt the ever so chatty students. She cleared her throat and raised her voice.

"*Excuse me*, class, if you'd *like* to pay attention to the whiteboard, *please.*" The class settled down and turned their attention to Miss Clayton, who had her tongue in her cheek, one booted foot tapping on the linoleum floor.

Coral thought to herself that she would love to stay behind after class and give her teacher some tips on how to prevent extreme perspiration with the correct choice of clothing and deodorant. It was making her feel uncomfortable just watching her teacher get shinier by the second.

"Thank you. This project is, in fact, yours as individuals," she said. Coral gave a sigh of relief. "However, you must share your findings with your chosen partners. I want you to delve into a book or any piece of writing you can find, and you're looking for something that represents you and your thoughts, how you function as a person and how you see yourself in this world. Once you've found your piece of writing, discuss with your partner your findings. So, with that in mind, the lesson is now over, and I'm giving you free roam of the library and the computer suite to make a start on this project with your partners. Enjoy, and make the most of our resources while you still have them," she said and sat back down on her seat, causing it to squeak as it adjusted to the weight being dropped onto it, like a very large sack of potatoes.

The rest of the room shifted, and the sudden noises of packing up bags, papers and books filled the air, students scurrying out of the door to clearly do anything *but* what work they had just been set. Coral swiftly got up from her seat and made a beeline for the door, hearing quick footsteps behind her. As she sauntered down the hallway and through the doors into the sixth form common room, Molly circled in front of her and gave her a confused look.

"There won't be anywhere to research in here."

"I'm well aware of that, Sherlock Holmes," Coral said, smiling sarcastically, sidestepping Molly and taking a seat in her usual spot by the window that looked out over the school playing field and rolling hills in the distance. She wished so badly she was out there rather than in the stuffy humid school that felt more like a prison and had done every year that she'd had to endure being there. She was so close to finishing her final year of sixth form, she could almost smell the freedom and fresh air that she would get once she'd burst out of the front doors and into the real world. Instead, she scrunched up her nose in disgust at the smell of a microwave pizza cooking in the small kitchenette behind her. *Who could even eat that at this time of the day?* Coral wondered. It wasn't even 10 o'clock yet.

"The sooner we start the project, the better; you never know how long it could take to find something truly meaningful to us," Molly said, taking the seat facing Coral.

She was such a bubbly little specimen, the complete opposite to Coral, but she liked that, especially the effort she was making with her. *It couldn't hurt to have a new friend*, she thought, *or a minion at least*. Coral lolled her head over the back of the blue cushioned seat, closing her eyes tight, and then opened them up to see the tiled ceiling in her vision. Slowly positioning her head back to look at the everlasting smiling Molly, she sighed.

"Okay," Coral said as she slowly rose up from her seat, Molly's smile growing even wider, "you've persuaded me. Library or computer suite?"

* * * *

I should've known Molly would want to do the project old-school, Coral thought as she ran her fingers over the book spines, slowly making her way in-between the many rows of crammed bookshelves. How was she going to find a book that represented her out of all of the books in the library? *There is definitely no book as brilliant and messed up as me*, Coral thought. *Miss Clayton never said I couldn't write the book myself, though, so there's an idea…*

Her thoughts were interrupted by Molly, staggering over to her, struggling to carry a tower of books that hid her dimpled cheeks. "A… little… help… please," she helplessly gasped between her pursed lips, puffing and panting as the books slowly began to weigh her down.

Coral smirked at Molly before she decided to take half of the pile of books from her, which she did effortlessly as if they weighed next to nothing. They made their way over to a vacant table which had names deeply chiselled into them, which clearly would've taken much concentration, determination and hours using a very good pen or compass.

"I'm so excited to see what we find and what speaks to us from the books the most. I love reading so much," Molly squeaked with excitement, taking a seat at the table and beginning to organise the books into piles.

How could someone like Molly be paired up with someone like me? Coral wondered. *We're complete opposites.*

Coral snatched up a book with a bright green cover and gold leaves embedded in it. She flicked through a few pages before landing on one, closing her eyes, and pointing at the middle of the page on the left-hand side, and went on to read it aloud. "In your darkest times, you will close up into a tight ball, but I promise, you will find yourself in those darkest hours, and you will be reborn."

Molly smiled up at her. "That sounds so inspiring, doesn't it?" she said, flicking through the pink-bound book she had in her hands.

"Doesn't it just," Coral murmured. *This is going to be one hell of a long-winded project*, Coral thought.

* * * *

Coral made it home by four o'clock and went straight into the kitchen, grabbing her usual carton of grapefruit juice and a bag of tortilla chips and carrying them up the stairs to her room. She didn't show much interest in the books in the library, but the green gold-leafed book had caught her attention, as if it was speaking to her, which sounded crazy, but she blamed that on her lack of alcohol and craving for cigarettes. Coral quickly got changed into comfier clothes and then slid out her bottle of Jack Daniels from underneath her bed that Dylan had left from previous nights before. Getting herself comfy on her windowsill, she brought her knees up to her chest to balance the book on without it slipping onto the floor and started to read.

* * * *

After a few hours of reading the book and the Jack Daniels bottle almost empty but still tightly held in her grasp, her phone buzzed from across the room. She chose to ignore it, engrossed within her newfound book, but her phone went on to buzz again. Carefully edging her way off the windowsill, she picked up her phone and swiped to see who'd messaged her. A playful smile formed on her lips while she slipped her phone into the front pocket of her shorts, her hip stinging in response, causing her to flinch, reminding her of what she was trying to avoid. She hid the book she'd been flicking through in her bedside drawer to read again later.

"I can't avoid it forever," she said to herself, looking in the floor-length mirror at her reflection and the scratches and bruises on her thighs. "Looks like it's time to interrogate the boyfriend."

* * * *

Once the bus had dropped Coral off outside the flats, she walked up the single flight of stone stairs leading to the top level where Dylan lived. She was so grateful he didn't live at home with his parents still; she couldn't imagine having to climb up the back of a house and hide in a bedroom from *his* family. It wasn't a normal thing, but since when was life normal in *her* world?

As she raised her hand to the door, it opened before she had the chance to knock, and as she stepped through, she was greeted by a custard doughnut being shoved into her mouth or as close to as it would go. She laughed as it smushed all over her lips, luckily catching in her hands the remaining pieces that didn't make it into her mouth.

"Thanks," she mumbled, with a weary smile, as Dylan led her through the door and to the sofa.

"I treat you like the queen you are, well, the custard queen at least," he said, lighting a cigarette and pouring them each a drink, obviously the alcoholic kind.

She looked around the room as she settled down onto the worn-out sofa, eyeing up the empty takeaway boxes piled up by the bin, the mountain of dirty dishes in the sink and the thick layer of dust on almost every surface. Dylan wasn't perfect, far from it, but he was one of the few distractions in Coral's life that she needed the most.

"How was school?" he asked, putting her feet in his lap and stroking her legs, giving her a devilish grin.

"Please don't call it school. You make me sound so young," she said while stretching out to her full length. She was so tired; all that reading from earlier, which she wasn't used to doing, had knocked it out of her. "But anyway, it was okay, usual rubbish, but I made a new friend, so that's decent at least."

"New friend?" Dylan asked, taking a long drag on his cigarette and blowing the smoke out like a chimney.

"A girl called Molly; she's in my English Literature class, and we're doing a project together; she chose me as her project partner."

"Ooh, sounds *very* exciting," he remarked sarcastically, moving his fingers further up her legs.

"More exciting than *your* day, I bet," she retorted. "How many hours of gaming did you waste entertaining yourself today?" Coral smirked, taking a big swig of her drink, sighing at the instant buzz it gave her as it burned down her throat; she'd waited all day for that feeling.

"Well, I'd waste more hours on you if you skipped school more," he said and smirked back, winking at her.

"Hey," she said, kicking out at him, "*waste?*"

He squeezed her knees gently. "You know I'm only joking. Now put that drink down and come here." As Coral got up to straddle him, he held up a finger, meaning to wait. "Hold on. I needed to ask, what's the deal between you and the tanned sleazebag?"

Sleazebag? Coral recoiled at this.

"You'll have to be a bit more specific, seeing as I don't know anyone as sleazy as you."

Dylan took yet another long hard drag on his cigarette and proceeded to blow out like a chimney in her face, causing her to scrunch up her nose.

"I'm not sure of his name, but you were getting pretty cosy with him at the engagement party." Coral had no recollection of the night of the engagement party, but she knew she had bad bruises and scratches from that night. Maybe he had caused them. She didn't want to ruin the mood, but Dylan was the one who'd brought this up, and she knew she had to confront him on it sometime.

"Is that why you gave me the bruising and scratches?" she asked, slowly moving away and perching on the coffee table in front of him. Now he was the one to recoil, but then he looked down into his lap.

"You weren't listening to me."

"And what was I not listening to you say?" Coral asked, taking a sip of her drink, never removing her gaze from him. He slowly looked up at her, locking eyes, and then searched her face.

"You got that drunk you can't remember?"

"Maybe there was a hidden ingredient in my drink that made me forget," she retorted sharply, all playfulness gone. She got up and moved to the door. *No point in sticking around when he's being a complete arsehole,* she thought.

Dylan quickly got up and grabbed her wrist. "Coral, wait, don't go. I'm being a knob. I was just jealous, that's all. He was making sure you were okay, and I was too fixed on my anger towards him to think about you and how you were, which I know sounds lame, but it's all I've got. I'm sorry; please come back." He trailed a finger up her arm making her shiver. "We can watch *Resident Evil*? I know you love those films."

He gently pulled her over to the sofa once more, and they both sat down together as he wrapped his arms around her and pulled her in for a long deep kiss. He always got what he wanted in the end, but she wasn't so sure that she did.

* * * *

Coral stirred and stared at the alarm clock across Dylan's bedroom. *Shit,* she thought. It read just after three o'clock in the morning. Time had fast-forwarded so quickly since they'd watched the film and made their way to his room. She slowly sat up, pulling the duvet around her while squinting into the darkness, searching for her clothes. Swinging her legs over the edge of the bed, she padded around the room, first finding her bra, clipping the hooks around her back, then her shorts which she slid on easily, making sure not to press into the bruising.

Then she searched until she found her knickers in the corner of the room behind a wastepaper bin, but pocketed them quickly as she already had her shorts on and needed to get home as soon as possible. She hadn't realised that he'd thrown them that far when he'd tugged them off her, but then again, things had gotten hot and steamy pretty quickly, so she wouldn't have been paying much attention. Once she found her t-shirt and had it on, she grabbed his navy-blue hoodie, slid it over her head and tiptoed out of the room, closing the door behind her. Quickly making her way across the carpeted floor, she slid her feet into her trainers, ready for the trail home and left the flat without a trace.

****

By the time she'd got home and climbed through her bedroom window, it was some time past four o'clock. *School is going to be so rough tomorrow*, she thought, slipping out of her clothes and into her oversized nightshirt. Just as she was about to climb into her bed, she walked over to her shorts and took the underwear out, ready to wriggle back into them, but something didn't feel right.

Flicking the switch on her bedside lamp, she held the underwear close enough to the light to reveal the luminous green lacy knickers in her hand. Coral quickly unclenched her fingers, causing the scant material to drop to the floor. She detested luminous colours with a passion. So, whose knickers were they?

6

"So, Coral, how are you feeling today?" Yasmin asked, moving her hip-length salt and pepper hair away from her monolid shaped eyes.

"Apart from feeling completely exhausted from lack of sleep and life itself, I'm doing okay." Coral had been going to see her therapist, Yasmin, since she was 14; her promise to her dad if her grief-stricken world and recklessness hadn't been resolved even the tiniest amount. Half the time, she believed her dad should've been getting help too, but instead he barricaded himself away in his room. Coral did what she could for him by continuing to attend therapy after all these years, even if it never got any easier. She enjoyed her sessions with Yasmin, always feeling comforted and at peace, finding she could relate to her in some ways. Yasmin had told her many years ago that she too had lost her mum, but in a car accident that was later proven deliberate, so she enjoyed conversing with her, knowing she felt somewhat the same sort of pain as she had been suffering and therefore would understand the loss of a mother.

"Have you had trouble sleeping since our last session?" Yasmin asked, sitting back in her padded plum-coloured armchair. Coral shook her head and crossed one leg over the other.

"I saw Dylan Wednesday night and must've nodded off by accident, so I didn't get home till late. I didn't have any battery power left in my phone either, so I couldn't ring for a taxi and had to walk home, so I'm still catching up on my sleep from then."

She decided to spare the details of finding another girl's underwear in his bedroom and taking them home accidentally, as well as freaking out over why he'd physically hurt her. She was deliberating even mentioning the underwear situation to Dylan but knew she had to; it was the right thing to do. Coral wouldn't be taken for a fool, not even because of him and his potential inability to be loyal.

"Ah yes, young love, I remember those days, although it was more difficult for me. You see, we didn't have mobile phones when I met Ivan, so it was always a risk sneaking to see each other in the still of the night." She smiled fondly at the memory replaying in her mind.

"I can imagine mine and Dylan's relationship is *extremely* different to yours and your husband's, Yasmin. Trust me; he doesn't have a romantic bone in his body. We just keep each other sane in dark times, and that's about it really," Coral said, leaning forward for her glass of water. It saddened her sometimes, knowing Dylan took her for a joy ride rather than a lifetime relationship, but what did she expect? He was just as broken as she was, so it was hardly going to go anywhere in the long run; it was clearly just until one of them crossed the finish line, claiming victory in being mentally stable again, but who would win that race?

Yasmin looked down, still smiling. "Don't all couples?" She reconnected their eye contact. "How are you feeling about this afternoon's plans?"

Coral took a deep, steady breath and looked away. "Not as bad as I usually do. I ordered some beautiful yellows and oranges for the arrangement as they were her favourite colours, so I'm looking forward to collecting them."

"Well, I'm sure she'll love them, Coral. She'd be very proud of you with the progress you've made and the progress you continue to make every day," Yasmin said, cutting a slice of blackcurrant cake, sliding it onto a plate and passing it to Coral; their shared favourite cake. Who'd have thought she'd share so many common interests with an East Asian therapist in her late forties.

"I should hope so. I spend enough money on them for her," Coral joked. Yasmin laughed lightly, which sounded like a light tinkling noise as if a wind chime had moved in the breeze. "In other news, I don't smoke as much. Mainly because if I continue, by the time I'm 30, my lungs will have packed up and I'll look way older than I actually am. I can't be having that. I want to be young forever."

"I used to say the same, but my hair and the wrinkles starting to form on my face give my age away, unfortunately," Yasmin said, breaking off some of her slice of cake, popping it into her mouth, and chewing softly.

"I've told you before, I'll happily dye your hair for you if you want; I've become some sort of an expert with hair dye," Coral said, flicking her bright hair dramatically off of her shoulder. "The roots are definitely starting to show my blonde, though. Oh yeah, I forgot to mention," Coral said, putting down her plate, "I was watching a television show about a girl who'd lost her brother in a house fire, and I realised just how much I had in common with her. She, too, lost someone she loved to a greater force than she could reckon with when she was a child, like I had as a child too. But now I'm older, I feel like I'm learning to understand it more, if that makes sense?

"Like, I can sort of understand maybe what my mum was feeling when she decided to do what she did. She was suffering for who knows what reason, but it was such a great force that it drove her to the edge. Pun accidental." She leant forward for her plate and took a bite of her cake, chewed for a few moments, then swallowed hard. "I mean, I won't deny it; grieving sucks more than anything, and I wouldn't wish it on my worst enemy. It must get easier by such a teeny tiny fraction, so miniature that you don't even notice it. I do still explode with anger and frustration from time to time because of it, and my insides feel like they've rotted away from all the damage I've done, but I'm not letting the loss of my mum define me as much these days. Well, that's what I want to believe; what happens in reality is a whole different ball game. I just try not to blame myself as much anymore."

Yasmin smiled at Coral from behind her cup of tea, placed it on the coffee table and started to smooth out the bohemian styled dress she was wearing. "Like I said, Coral, your mum would be very proud of you."

* * * *

Once the therapy session had come to an end, Coral reluctantly got up and left, sauntering down the path leading away from Yasmin's office and out of the white gate, admiring the flowers as she walked past. *Another place that makes me feel alive*, she thought, *and the closest I have to a conversation with another mother figure*. Yasmin had become such a big part of her life; she didn't know what she'd have done without her, without these chats with blackcurrant cake and cups of tea.

* * * *

Luckily for Coral, the florist wasn't too far from Yasmin's home, so she happily walked there, taking in the comforting feeling of the warm sun on her skin and the clear blue sky above her. If one thing was for sure, she was grateful for growing up in such a beautiful village, surrounded by exquisite nature. It made up for the lack of beauty growing inside of her or within her home; beauty hadn't existed in those places in a very long time.

The people who walked by her didn't seem to be in a hurry: women strolling with their happy gurgling babies in their prams, dog walkers and those just exercising in general, but even they took it at a leisurely pace. Nothing was quick about the village, and that's just the way she liked it, nice and steady like life should be. She'd be ruined if she lived in the city, just the thought of loud noises, cars left, right and centre, people in suits marching from one place to another with briefcases in one hand and mobile phones attached like Velcro between a raised hand and their ears; it was enough to make her feel sick and put her off for life.

* * * *

After she had collected the flowers, her legs took her in a dream-like daze to where she needed to be, and before she could make sense of where she was, the big iron gates loomed in front of her, creaking slightly whenever a strong breeze bustled through. Coral gripped the bunch of flowers tightly in her hand and made her way across the paved ground, looking at all the headstones as she steadily walked past them. There were flowers at nearly all the headstones, some fresh and bright, others wilting or completely lifeless. One headstone she hadn't seen before was that of what she gathered was a little boy; blue ribbons and teddy bears scattered in front of it, making her heart wrench. He was only six years old and taken too early, it read, but now he was an angel in heaven with his daddy and sister.

So tragic, Coral thought. She didn't go straight to her mum's headstone but instead sat on a nearby bench that read: 'Margery Mabelstone: 1950 - 2017. Lived a long and happy life. Forever missed'.

"I hope you don't mind me joining you, Margery. I just need a moment."

Seeing that little boy's headstone had triggered something in Coral, and a few tears squeezed out from her closed eyes in response. Growing up, especially when her mum had died, she couldn't quite grasp death and who decided who was taken at what age and how. It still confused her and made her feel unsettled now, but she had to do what brought her some form of comfort about it all. Reading headstones and seeing what lay in front of them made her feel strange but closer to 'the other side' as some called it. She'd never had any experience with the afterlife and quite frankly didn't want to, but it didn't stop her belief that there was one. She hoped her mum was happy and free in that place and not as unhappy as she was on earth in their little home.

Despite what she had told Yasmin, Coral would forever blame herself for not being enough of a good daughter; no matter how many times family and friends told her to not blame herself, she couldn't help it. Why couldn't she see the sadness in her mum's eyes, the downward shape of her lips or the tear-stained cheeks she'd kiss when she left for school every morning? None of those things had ever shown in her mum. If there was ever any depression within her mum, she was very good at hiding it from herself and the rest of her family. She had always been so happy and joyful, even on the day she'd decided to take a one-way ticket to the lake and off the face of the earth. She'd promised to make butterfly buns with her at the weekend and help her paint for her art project about the seaside. How could she make all these empty promises if she knew she'd never be around to keep them?

Coral felt ashamed for not recognising the signs, no matter how well hidden they must have been, but if she felt this low about it, she couldn't imagine how her dad had felt and clearly did still feel. Even though she hardly felt as if she knew her dad at all these days, she knew the feeling of grief and loss was something they both had in common; and she knew Kruze felt exactly the same. All three of them would take that pain to their death bed; the uncertainty of what happened that day would forever haunt them.

"Thank you, Margery," Coral said, patting the bench, wiping at the stray tears holding steady on her cheeks, "but I must go do my duty now."

As Coral leant forward, her legs didn't move an inch, as if her feet were glued to the very spot in which they were placed on the ground beneath her. *Maybe Margery wants a chat,* Coral thought. She had all the time in the world. Some could find it strange, but to her, it would bring her some well-needed comfort while she had no one else around to talk to.

"Margery, I'm struggling... I truly am. But I'm trying for her. I want her to be proud of me, even though I have well and truly fucked up; excuse my language, I'm expressing myself. Every day is the biggest struggle. I just can't seem to shake it off and get on with life. I don't want to abuse my body like I do. It makes me happy till I'm home alone in my bedroom, waiting for the next scenario, so I can take a drag or raise a shot glass to my lips... and I really don't want to do that anymore... I just don't know how to stop..." she trailed off. Coral rose up from the bench, wiping a few more stray tears from her face, and picked up the flowers next to her that she'd got for her mum.

"Till the next time, Margery," she said and began walking again, carefully placing her feet one in front of the other and looking at her flowers. They were stunning and so bright in colour, a perfect representation of who her mum was. Coral was the only one who ever made an effort for the headstone on behalf of herself, her dad and Kruze; the only one who could withstand coming here, the only flowers to be laid down in remembrance every year. No matter the cost, she'd always make sure it was a sight worth seeing to honour her mum.

As she wound her way in and out of the headstones, she caught sight of her mum's, but as she edged closer to the grave, she felt her legs buckle beneath her and fell uncomfortably onto the soft grass. Rubbing her eyes, she slowly crawled over on her hands and knees to her mum's grave, still clutching her flowers. Her body felt like a dead weight, and so she could only inch forward slightly; she felt the same as she had the day after the lake party. Forcing herself to look up, she got the sensation of her heart stopping beating for a few moments, then felt it pick up a tremendous speed all of a sudden. She placed a hand on her chest as if her heart was about to puncture through her and cause a gaping hole.

"What... the... hell..." she gulped for air as her sentence drifted out of her mouth and off into the humid air around her. Her eyes clocked something unfamiliar to her. Ever since her mum had passed, she was the only one who had ever laid flowers on her grave, and yet this time, there, beneath the headstone, lay a cheap bunch of supermarket flowers with the price still on. They were white and purple, clearly not her favourite colour, so whoever had got them hadn't even given her mum a single thought and done it on a whim; that's if they were even placed at the right headstone.

"Who would even put these here? They're clearly in the wrong place. If you want something doing..." Coral murmured to herself, anger beginning to course through her veins as she twisted over the tag attached to one of the stems to read what it said. Coral snatched her hand away as if the tag had scalded her skin, and her stomach dropped as if she'd just done the first loop of a rollercoaster, acid rising up into her throat, making her double over and choke it out. Gingerly, she looked at the tag one more time and read it out loud.

"I'm sorry for what I did. I miss you. I love you, Cammy."

7

Tearing through rows and rows of headstones, Coral couldn't get away quick enough. She'd abandoned the beautiful flowers she'd brought with her and left them where she'd dropped them at her mum's grave, speeding off in a state of turmoil, acid slowly rising up through her chest and to her throat again; it took all of her strength to keep it at bay. Holding her phone high above her head, waving her arm frantically, Coral tried with all her might to get a couple of signal bars on her phone in her state of panic; if anyone saw her from a distance, they'd probably think she was trying to run with an imaginary kite. So many alarm-stricken thoughts raced around her mind. *Who would've left the flowers on my mum's grave, and what on earth did those words on the tag even mean?*

Finally, finding one bar of signal on her phone and another one flickering to give her hope, she clicked on Iris's name and the 'call' button. Impatiently tapping her foot on the dry earth beneath her, while the long-overdue tears stung her eyes, she hoped Iris would answer on the first ring. However, when she didn't answer after three phone calls, she tried one last time, and Iris luckily picked up straight away. By this point, the tears had spread faster than she could anticipate down her face, leaving traces of black eyeliner staining her cheeks. She knew she looked like something from a horror movie, which was quite ironic being in a cemetery.

"Three missed phone calls. What's going on?" Iris asked breathlessly down the phone. "I was in a meeting and it's just finished. Are you okay? Where are you?"

"Iris, you need... to come here... quickly. I'm... at the... cemetery," she frantically and breathlessly got out the words, panic rising in her chest, causing bile to hit her throat at full force now, trying its best to escape out of her mouth. Doubling over just in time for the acid to spill out, she dropped her phone in the process. This was new for Coral; she hadn't felt such heart-wrenching fear coursing through her since she was 13, finding out the sickening news for the first time. It was like déjà vu.

Coral swiped at her phone and placed it back to her ear, just in time to hear Iris say, "What's happened? Do I need to get a speeding ticket for this emergency or what?" Coral could hear Iris's heels clicking against the ground of the car park where her work was and the loud *thunk* sound from pulling on her car door.

"Just get here as soon as possible, please," she choked out and hung up, the floodgates opening fully, letting the tears stream down her face even more, along with more bile setting free from her throat and onto the grass beneath her. In all the years of suffering she'd gone through, this was like the cherry on top of the most heartbreaking disastrous cake ever to be created. Her body was shaking as if she were standing barefoot in the snow rather than in over twenty-degree heat. Someone leaving flowers for her mum wasn't what had shaken her; it was the words that were written on the tag. Clearly, she wasn't the only one mourning her mum's anniversary today. But what had the person said sorry for? What had they done to her mum to still be saying sorry, even after she'd left this world?

* * * *

What felt like hours but was merely a matter of dragged-out double-figure minutes, Coral sat on the grass, trying her best to control her breathing. She felt as though she was suffocating on a normal day, but this was too much, and the taste of unwanted bile was still plastered to her taste buds making her feel even worse. Coral heard Iris bounding towards her and suddenly felt herself get scooped up off of the ground. Iris threw her arms around her best friend and squeezed so tight that Coral could feel the remaining oxygen draining from her lungs, causing her to slump slightly, but she didn't care. It was what she needed right now, and if it caused her pain, then so be it. They stood there in the baking heat like that for quite some time, Coral sobbing onto Iris's bare shoulder, making it glisten with her murky tears in the sunlight as well as sticky with sweat.

In a caring manner, Iris peeled Coral off and held her at arm's length; her manicured fingers gripped both shoulders as she looked deep into her eyes. It was something she'd done when Coral had first found out about her mum; their bond got stronger every day after that, giving them a connection like no other friendship ever had in their lives. It was as if Coral's eyes were crystal balls, and Iris was staring into them, trying to find deeper meanings and explanations.

"Coral, get your breath back and slowly explain to me what's happened to make you like… *this*," Iris said, looking horrified at the state Coral was in but trying to stay composed to some extent for the both of them.

Doing as she was told, she took a deep breath but couldn't get the words out, relaying the sentences in her head, none of them doing justice to what she'd seen and how she felt. With this in mind, Coral took Iris's hand and gently pulled, taking her back to the grave on very unsteady legs. She stopped a few headstones away and pointed a shaky finger towards her mum's grave. Iris looked at Coral, then back at the headstone.

"I don't understand?" she said, a questionable tone in her voice and looking back at Coral with pure concern on her face. "A bunch of flowers made you react like this?"

"Go... go read the tag on those... *cheap* flowers," Coral said, once again feeling as if she was being choked, struggling to get the oxygen into her lungs. Iris did as Coral said, looking mostly confused, and walked over, crouching down, making sure her black fitted skirt didn't touch the grass. Flipping the card over with her fingers, she stared at it for a short time before getting back up, holding a hand to her head with her eyes tightly closed shut. She always did this when something was clouding her mind and making her feel negative; Coral knew this well by now.

"*This* is what's upset you?" Iris asked.

Coral croaked out a "yeah" before picking up the flowers she'd got for her mum. She discarded the purple and white flowers behind the headstone, but not without pulling the tag from a stem, snapping it accidentally, placing the flowers she'd bought for her mum in front of the headstone. "I'm the only one who ever brings flowers on behalf of myself, Kruze and my dad, and it's been that way for years," she said, wiping a stray tear that slowly made its way down her cheek.

"I know," Iris said, taking Coral's hand and giving it a gentle squeeze. "Let's go back to mine, get a drink and have a proper talk about this with no one else around. Aaron and my mum are both at work for a solid three more hours at least, so we've got the house to ourselves until then. Come on," she said, gently pulling Coral behind her, "let's go."

Coral looked behind her, completely bewildered. Just when she thought she'd dealt with today quite well, something *always* had to ruin her progress.

* * * *

Iris pushed open the front door to her house, slipped off her shoes in the hallway, slid on her fluffy slippers, and headed straight over to the fridge. Coral closed the door behind her and took off her trainers, almost in slow motion, her head feeling beyond fuzzy, and her body feeling as if she were floating. Her mind had gone blank, and a whirl of grey spun around in her mind fogging everything around her.

To some, seeing another bunch of flowers on a grave would've given others a sense of gratitude and gratefulness. But this wasn't a normal bunch of flowers; they were soaked in guilt. Coral could smell it on them as soon as her eyes had left the tag that had been attached, which was now deeply rooted into her shorts' pocket.

As Iris placed two bottles of cider down on the kitchen island and opened them, Coral hopped onto a bar stool and took a big swig of the drink. However, it didn't give her the buzz she usually felt; it just fizzed around the numbness within her, which in turn made her feel more sick. Iris hopped onto the bar stool opposite her, and gestured for the tag. Dragging it out of her shorts pocket and gently placing it on the kitchen island top, Coral shivered. She didn't get a good feeling from the tag that had been attached to the flowers, not one little bit. The fact they were apologising drove her anger forwards; she wanted to know who had written on the tag and interrogate them at all costs as to why they were so sorry towards her deceased mum.

"Right, we both know the words written on the tag, so we don't need to read it aloud over and over again; it won't help. However, we *do* need to interpret what it could mean. Do you feel okay to do that?" Iris asked, looking up at Coral. She nodded hesitantly, and they both looked at the writing on the tag.

"Well," Iris said after a few minutes of speculating, "it's clearly stating about someone who feels guilty about something they did or said when your mum was alive that could've potentially hurt her feelings. Maybe this person didn't apologise and wishes they had done, and after five years, has finally done something about it that brings them some form of comfort and peace. That's what I get from it anyway."

Iris took a long drink from her bottle and then hopped off her seat, grabbing a chocolate bar from the cupboard and breaking it up into a small glass bowl. Coral watched her in awe. One minute she was in a business meeting, the next being somewhat of a grievance counsellor, and then playing detective with her. *What a woman she is in comparison to me,* Coral thought.

"Have you got any thoughts?" Iris asked, placing the bowl between them and popping a piece of chocolate into her mouth.

Coral had been thinking about her mum's death rather than the tag the entire time she'd been sitting in her seat, but this was something that occurred regularly for her and had done ever since the day she was told they'd found her mum. Nothing mattered to her more than trying to understand the reason behind her mum's death and what made her do it. Sometimes, she couldn't believe the honest truth: her mum had been suicidal for some time and chose to leave this world and her beautiful family behind, the sadness buried deep within her clearly too strong to live with.

"Maybe the honest truth hasn't been so honest after all," Coral thought out loud. It never had sat comfortably with her, even after all these years; the pieces of the puzzle of her mum's final day on earth so unclear, not fitting together correctly as if the pieces were being forced to fit.

"What do you mean?" Iris asked, confusion still etching her face.

"So," Coral started, picking at the skin on the side of her thumb, "hear me out. The police said my mum died of suicide. Everyone accepted it and moved on, but *I* didn't. I blamed myself for years because apparently her evil thoughts took her, and I never noticed a change in her. But what if she *didn't* have evil thoughts? I mean, I've had evil thoughts for years, and I haven't done anything about it yet."

Iris looked at her from beneath her fanned-out eyelashes and simply nodded, leaning forward and listening intently.

"Maybe what happened to my mum wasn't due to the evil thoughts or a tragic death from her hand... maybe it was something else that took her away."

Coral looked at Iris to see her contemplating what had been said, but then her eyebrows knitted together, and she took another drink from her bottle and said, "I'm not following."

Coral cleared her throat, shaky with what she was about to say. "Well, my mum was taken from me when I was 13 by suicide. Now I'm 18, and after I found this tag attached to the flowers on her grave... Well, what if my mum's life wasn't taken by her own hands? What if someone had a vendetta against her and..." She couldn't bear to finish the sentence, from both the fear of making it real and admitting to the possibility but also the fear of Iris thinking she'd lost her mind completely today.

Iris didn't say a word for a few minutes, and then she broke the silence. "That's one hell of an accusation, Coral," she near enough mumbled. "Have you ever thought of this before today?"

"Yeah, I have, but I was young and had a wild imagination and wanted a real reason why she'd died, not just one the police summoned up. But I'm not young anymore, and I still refuse to believe that the woman I called my mum would abandon us when I know how happy she was with life; she *loved* life, Iris. It makes no sense why she'd leave it all behind." Coral sat forward and picked up a piece of chocolate. "I know it's a big accusation to make, and I'm not making it lightly, but think about it for a moment. She was so happy all the time, everyone loved her; even on the day she was found dead, she'd already told me in the morning that we could make butterfly buns together at the weekend. There's no way she'd make an empty promise like that to me."

Iris sat listening and didn't say a word, so Coral continued.

"How can it make sense that one day, randomly, she chooses to end it all and leave her perfect world behind. It never added up back then, and it still doesn't. The police just put two and two together when they found the knife with her blood and DNA on and her wrists slit, but who's to say that's what happened. I didn't believe it then, and I still don't, Iris. Call me crazy or a lunatic or whatever; have me sent off to a crazy house. The writing on this tag could be the start of what I thought all along, and it could end where we *really* find out what happened to her."

Iris stared at her, and Coral couldn't tell what her best friend was thinking. Probably that she was completely insane; she thought that about herself most of the time too. "Have you mentioned it to Kruze before? These thoughts on what you think could've happened to your mum?" she asked Coral, picking at the label on her bottle.

"How could I? I wouldn't have had a clue how to bring it up in conversation with him; I struggle at times as it is with normal life."

"I think it'd be worth talking to him about it or even talking to Yasmin about how you feel. She could potentially shed some light on it from her perspective of how the mind works after trauma has happened in someone's life. But Kruze should know your thoughts on this. He's your brother and works in the force; at least then he'll know whether or not to mention the tag to the police."

Coral coughed as she took a sip of her drink in response to the word police.

"Police?" she'd not even considered mentioning the tag to the police. Then again, she had no idea what her next step would be in this; after all, it was just a thought. It had taken her this long to build up the courage to mention it to Iris, let alone anyone else, but the tag on the flowers had prompted her.

"Well yeah, obviously. It could be prime evidence of someone in relation to what you think could've happened. Mention it to Kruze, see what he says on the matter, and we'll take it from there," Iris said. "That's all we can do for now, really; like I say, it's a big accusation to make, especially after so much time has passed and only basing your thoughts on this tag. Can you think of anyone who would even have a vendetta against your mum?"

Coral puffed out her cheeks and shrugged her shoulders. "No one," Coral murmured but then reconsidered. "But then again, I was only 13 when she died; I wasn't really paying attention to things like that. The only people she really came into contact with often were her clients."

Coral's mum had had a booming gardening business before she died; many people in the village came to their home to marvel at their garden and ask for a price list from her. She loved gardening and always took pride in her work, not stopping until a project was perfectly done, giving it all of her love and attention, no matter how long it took her; gardening was practically the third child in her life or a second husband.

"You could see if she had a clientele book or something along those lines," Iris suggested, draining her bottle and placing it down carefully on the kitchen island top. "I can guarantee she will have done. She was always organised; I admired that quality in her."

Just as Coral was about to reply, Luciana stepped through the door, bags of shopping in tow, swinging behind her in her tightly gripped hands with her freshly polished nails.

"You're home early," Iris said, making Luciana jump, showing she was completely unaware that anyone was already home. Iris hopped down to help her mum with the bags of shopping.

"My goodness, Carena, you nearly put me in an early grave," she said, then dropped the bags and held her hands up to her mouth once she'd noticed Coral sat at the kitchen island. "Beautiful girl. I am so sorry, I didn't mean—"

Coral held up her hands once she'd hopped down from the bar stool to help. "Luciana, it's fine. I know you didn't mean anything by it."

Luciana pulled her into a tight hug, stroking her hair. "Are you staying for dinner?" she asked, pulling away and reaching for a shopping bag to unpack.

"As much as I'd usually say yes, I should really be home tonight with my brother and hopefully my dad. Thank you, though."

Coral gave Iris a quick hug and told her she'd drop her a text later. As she left, Aaron started to walk up the path holding a big bouquet of red roses. He raised a hand to Coral but didn't say a word, and she responded with a tight smile and a small wave back. He knew today was a hard day for her, so she was grateful for the gesture of kindness at least.

Walking away from Iris's house was normally a stab in the chest, but today it felt like she'd been hit by a bus. *Hopefully that feeling will become my reality,* she thought glumly, sauntering down the road, making her way back to her soul-draining home once again. The day may have been twenty-degree heat before, but now it felt as though she was walking through a blizzard to her igloo cold home, her body tensing at what was to come and the emotions that would follow in a painful pursuit.

8

The thick grief-filled air polluted Coral's lungs as she entered her front door. As she closed it behind her, she leant against the door, slowly sinking to the floor, gathering her knees up to her chest and taking long deep breaths. *Maybe if I sit here long enough, the wooden floorboards will swallow me up,* Coral thought, *and then both the constant pain in my chest and my own being will cease to exist.* But Coral was well aware that was just a sad reality of wishful thinking.

Gathering herself up off of the floor, Coral dragged herself up the stairs and looked towards one of the doors on the landing: the office door. The office was made for her parents so they could do their work in peace without Kruze and Coral disturbing them and barging in. If she was quiet enough, she could probably sneak in without being heard, not like her dad would step out of his room and tell her to get out, but she didn't want to risk it, especially today of all days.

Coral pushed on the unlocked door and stepped into the dust-congested room. It was big enough for two identical desks which possessed two old-fashioned computers on top, two chairs with wheels protruding from all angles tucked underneath, and a narrow bookcase in the corner. She covered her mouth as she tiptoed through the room, not wanting to suck the thick dusty air into her lungs too much; she felt like she was suffocating enough, she didn't need anything to add to that. Just like the rest of the house, the wallpaper was peeling horrendously, but then again, this room hadn't been entered, to her knowledge, since her dad stopped leaving his room, so why would it have been cared for when they could only just manage to care for themselves?

The light in the room was a mere flicker of an old bulb on its last spark, so Coral moved through the drawers in her mum's desk quickly and quietly, and after checking the last drawer, she found what she was looking for along with a few old family photos and a charm of a telephone box from her mum's missing charm bracelet. Two charms down, a whole bracelet to go.

Just as she left and closed the door behind her and began to enter the threshold to her bedroom, she heard a noise unfamiliar to her, yet it felt like a glimmer of something from her memories. It was only a gentle noise, but it was enough to slow her heart rate and make her hold her breath so she could listen intently to the plucking of her dad's guitar strings. Striding into her bedroom, she placed the notebook she'd found under her pillow and walked back to her doorway to listen to her dad continuing to pluck the strings and make beautiful sounds. For a second, Coral forgot all about the darkness in her heart and felt light as a feather, as if she were floating among the clouds.

As she closed her eyes and leant up against the door frame, she heard a wrong string being plucked, making a strangled sort of noise, and as quickly as she heard the string being plucked, the sound of wood repeatedly crashing down on wood filled her ears. Before she had time to think, Coral had leapt forward and was pounding on her dad's bedroom door, begging him to stop. Astounded with what she'd done, she slowly backed up from the door, the only noise being the creaking floorboards underneath her feet. The door to her dad's bedroom slowly creaked open, just a crack, but enough for her to see a few inches of him and his rugged face. Exhaustion riddled his features, she could see that clear as day, with the deep blue and grey bags under his eyes and how his previous designer stubble was now a thick wiry beard of carelessness. He cleared his throat before speaking, but it didn't help much to hide the huskiness of his voice.

"Sorry," her dad croaked out and cleared his throat again. "It didn't hold sentimental value anyway. It was just the replacement for the last one I..." he trailed off, swinging the door open fully to reveal the completely destroyed guitar lying shattered on the floorboards of his room. He looked at her face and then quickly looked away, recognising how frightened she'd been but not wanting to believe he could make her feel that way. "Sorry for scaring you. I didn't know you were home."

Coral stood up straight and gave a tight smile. "You didn't scare me. I was just enjoying... hearing you play. I haven't heard or seen you in a while. It was nice." With that, he looked up carefully and gave her a small smile. "Are you coming downstairs tonight?" she asked, hopeful as always.

"Kruze mentioned outside the door about making ravioli," Coral's dad said, "well, that *he* was going to make it. I'm not sure how that'll turn out, but it's not like I have anywhere to be if I get food poisoning," he said, breathing heavily and giving an empty noise that sounded somewhat of a lifeless chuckle at his own half-hearted humour.

Coral wondered when the last time was that he'd left the house to get fresh air or even left the room to get a shower. She opened her mouth to say something but thought better of it.

"What did you want to say?" he asked, stepping forward and closing the door behind him, making Coral stumble back slightly, startled at how calm he was keeping during their snippet of socialisation as if this was a normal occurrence for them. This rugged-looking man in front of her was her dad, and it wasn't easy to process. *You look so old,* Coral thought, trying to fight back the tears that were forming at the sight of what her dad had become after all these years. Grief works its magic on people in different ways; some dye their hair bright colours, and some gain untameable Viking beards and wrinkles.

"Nothing," Coral murmured, anxiety prickling up the back of her neck, "I'll see you downstairs." Spinning around on the heel of her foot, she skittered into her bedroom, gently shutting the door behind her and then slumped onto the seat at her dressing table, rubbing her eyes with the palms of her hands, looking at the black residue left behind from her eyes. Plucking out a makeup wipe, she set to work on her face. Her dad hadn't even commented about her makeup-stained cheeks and red-rimmed eyes, as if that was how every girl her age should look; a new fashion trend, perhaps.

Even though it had been a fleeting moment with her dad, it had knocked the air out of her lungs, and she felt exhausted as if she'd just finished a workout regime. All she wanted to do was tell him what was going on in her life, how she felt, and how much she missed him. But that was a big thing to do, and she didn't feel ready, not today of all days, but she wasn't sure when she'd next see him outside of his room again to tell him these things.

Once she'd heard her dad reach the bottom step and trudge into one of the downstairs rooms in the house, Coral picked up her phone and rang Iris. She picked up straight away on the first ring, probably terrified of missing another one of Coral's breakdowns of the day.

"Hey, did you find anything at home?" Iris asked, clearly chewing something and listening to music in the background.

"Yeah, I did," Coral said, sliding the notebook out from underneath her pillow, rapidly flicking through the pages. "I found a tatty notebook with a sticker on the front saying gardening clientele. I've just had a thought, though."

"That's good; at least you found something. What're you thinking?"

"Well," Coral started, "there are a few names that keep cropping up through the pages. Obviously, I haven't had a proper look, but we could always maybe... go see these people? I know it sounds stupid, crazy even, but I just don't want to bother Kruze with all of this, bringing it back up again—"

"It doesn't sound stupid. I mean, it sounds risky, and again, you're basing this off of words you found attached to flowers... but I do understand why you don't want to mention it to Kruze for the time being. Last thing your family needs is all this hassle with the case being opened up again, or even you getting hurt if the police just ignore what evidence you bring to them," Iris said, once again, crunching in Coral's ear. "Don't be hasty, though; this is serious, and we need to really think this through. This isn't some cartoon crime scene investigation where it gets solved in a wacky way that ends up working out in favour of the good guys. This is *real* life, Coral. This is *your* real life, and so we've got to tread delicately. The people in that clientele book might seem innocent on the outside, but one wrong word said to them and they could detonate. We don't know who we're dealing with."

Coral knew that Iris was right; this wasn't like in the films she watched where the evidence pops out from nowhere and the crime is finally solved. For all Coral knew, she could be completely wrong with her train of thought, and it could simply be that her mum *did* just want out of the real world. However, that didn't mean she was going to give up so easily; she just had to use her adult brain instead of the childlike brain that was latched onto a thought she'd conjured up from years gone by.

"I'll think about it all tonight, and I'll pick you up first thing in the morning, and we'll go for the Saturday special at Sunny Side Up, okay? Then we can go over everything and decide what steps to take while enjoying a full English breakfast. Does that sound like a plan?"

Coral gave a small smile to herself. "Sounds perfect; I'll see you then. Just text me when you know a time."

"I shall do. Now, you go spend the evening with your family and try and get some well-deserved rest tonight; you've had a tough day. Hang in there, girl, you've got this," Iris said and then hung up.

Coral flopped back onto her bed and let out a tremendous sigh. How had her day started off so productive with Yasmin and then ended up like this? All these years of plodding along through the mess her life had become, for it to now spiral even more out of control than it already had and send her spinning along with it.

"Who would want to hurt you, mum?" Coral whispered aloud while stroking the front of the clientele book. Even though the only thing to make her think it wasn't suicide after all this time was the tag on the flowers, which was probably a ridiculous thing for her to have broken down over anyway, it was enough to fuel her forwards into a new mindset.

Snapping back into reality, she realised just how weak her body felt and how her brain felt deflated. Right on cue, her stomach grumbled to add to it all. She needed food immediately and plenty of sleep; the sleep that never came, but she was sure as anything that after the day of crying rivers, she'd be out for the count within minutes once her head hit the pillow later.

Changing into her nightshirt and slipping on her worse for wear slippers, she carefully made her way down the stairs and into the kitchen, following the smell of pasta and sauce that was snaking its way up her nostrils.

9

The faded words of the shop 'Bloom With Me' sat on a sickly yellow sign above the grubby windows. The paint on the window edges was flecked and stained; the beautiful white it clearly was before was long gone and seemed like a lost cause, as well as the chipped mint green door. The only life that shone from this florist was the baskets of flowers out front by the door, beautiful variations of colours cascading from the hanging flower baskets at either side of the shop front. Whoever it was that ran this shop clearly had their heart in the right place; she'd seen it in her mum's arrangements at home, and as Coral and Iris entered the door, a bell lightly tinkling above their heads, she noticed that the styling of some of the bouquets looked quite familiar.

Over breakfast this morning, Coral had decided it was time to attempt to face some of her mum's potential demons or past clients going by the old notebook, and she was yet to decide whether demons was the correct term for them. There were many clients that dotted throughout her mum's clientele book; however, there were three names that popped up regularly, which she thought were more than just a coincidence: Daniella, Aunt Eva and Rodney. If she had no luck with these, she'd delve further, but for now, these were the three suspects she would be investigating.

As Coral looked around at the new environment she was in, she noticed that the walls were painted white and the floor a grubby beech wood, creaking under her boots as she slowly walked over to the counter where a woman, who looked to be in her late thirties, stood cutting stems on a current arrangement. Her faded honey-coloured hair tumbled down in front of her face as she concentrated on the task at hand, the whites of her knuckles showing under the dim lighting in the room. Without warning, icy blue eyes met Coral's, and for a split second, she thought she'd met this woman before and had the vaguest feeling of déjà vu again. But if this woman before her claimed to be the Daniella from her mum's clientele book, there's every chance she could've known Coral when she was a lot younger.

Despite the cold look in her eyes, the woman put down her secateurs and gave a friendly smile. "Hello there, girls," she said. Coral noticed that her voice had a slight huskiness to it, and she wasn't sure whether it was from hay fever, age or even tiredness, which was showing in the bags under her eyes. "What brings you to my little shop?"

"We're looking for a bouquet of reds and whites, any type of flower, for today if possible? Last-minute thing," Iris said. "My mum needs a pick-me-up."

"Of course." A small smile spread over her face, which showed she was trying to be polite and professional. "Any particular size?"

"I'll splash out and get her a large, boxed bouquet, please; saves any hassle. I'm not a novice at arranging flowers and neither is she," Iris said, smiling warmly at the woman, trying to make it as light and less awkward as possible.

Coral wasn't sure how she was going to start the conversation she needed to have. A wave of nausea washed over her as she realised that once upon a time, her own mum worked in this shop, probably when she was around Coral's age. As she put a hand to her head, the woman behind the counter did a double-take, and her eyes seemed to shine differently; she looked giddy if anything.

"Are you okay, honey? You don't seem too good," she said. "Let me go fetch you a glass of water." As the woman went out of the doorway behind her, Coral's eyes caught sight of a bunch of newspaper cuttings, posters and photo frames on the wall of the back room where the woman had gone through to. One of the photo frames in particular was that of two young women and a man in the middle, all smiling brightly with their arms wrapped around one another.

The woman sauntered back through the doorway with a glass of water and passed it to Coral. "There you go, drink up! It's probably dehydration with the heat outside; you girls need to keep up with your fluids when it's so hot."

"Thank you..." Coral murmured, taking a sip. It was rather refreshing and had a hint of lemon in it. "Sorry, I didn't catch your name."

The woman smiled, and her eyes gleamed once again. "I never offered it." Coral's eyebrows knitted together, but before she could ask again, the woman smiled and said, "I'm Daniella, but I think you already knew that." She walked back through the doorway and brought back the photo Coral had been staring at, closing the door behind her. "And I'm pretty certain you didn't want flowers from me today, did you?"

"Well—"

"It's okay. I knew this day would come. Yes, this man in the photograph is your dad, but no, we are not together, much to my dismay. I'm sure my life would've been a lot easier if I had been with him, but I'm sure your mum is a lovely woman, and she has nothing to worry about; I'm not looking to cause any trouble between them."

"I think you've got the wrong end of the stick here... and the wrong girl," Iris said, confusion pricking at her features; Coral could see this mix up had irritated her best friend.

"But... I saw you looking at the photo in the back there... I thought you were his daughter..." Daniella looked confused.

"I think," Coral said, pointing at the woman in the photo to the left of the man, "that *this* woman here was my mum."

Daniella's expression never changed. After a few moments passed of her staring at the photo, she locked eyes with Coral. There was a look on her face that Coral couldn't read. "Oh," Daniella whispered. Iris and Coral exchanged a glance, clearly unaware of how to comprehend her reaction. "I'm lost for words... I'm sorry... your mum was Cammy?" Daniella asked.

Coral flinched slightly at the use of her mum's name but not just that; it was the fact she'd called her Cammy. Not many people referred to her as that. It hadn't been used for so long and felt alien to her, causing her heart to instantly ache and feel like an anchor weighing her down.

"Yes, my mum was Camilla. How old would she have been in this photo?" Coral asked, hopeful for more information.

"Oh, she'd have been but a teen. Started here at 16 years old, just like me. We were best friends from the get-go; we just... clicked," she said and smiled in remembrance, clicking her fingers for extra effect. "Is that why you're here?"

Coral felt uncomfortable, all braveness and boldness seeping away. She needed to regain composure. "I was wondering if you could shed some light on any possible reasons as to why she would have wanted to kill herself." The words had tumbled out of Coral's mouth before she even had time to register what she had said, or at least before she had tried to put the words into a more tactful sentence.

Daniella placed a hand on her chest and widened her eyes. Taking a steady breath, she pulled out a stool from under the counter and perched on it. "Now that's winded me completely," she said, "the thought of her... No... she wouldn't have done that... she *loved* life. She *loved* everything." Daniella looked at Coral. "Your mum wouldn't have killed herself, I just know it. That just wouldn't make any sense."

"Well... can you think of..." Coral drifted from her sentence. How could she ask if there was anyone she might know that would have wanted to *kill* her mum? That was such a huge accusation, and it could put a huge spanner in the works with Daniella. At the end of the day, Coral didn't know her, and for all she knew, she could be lying.

"I mean, she had a loving family, a caring husband, and a thriving business... How could she have wanted to throw it all away?" Daniella asked, rubbing her eyes, but not enough to disrupt the dark charcoal eyeliner. Her words stung Coral, and it must have shown. "Oh no, honey, I didn't mean it like that, I just... It's hard to believe that someone who had everything would feel so down in this world to end it all, you know? It just doesn't add up."

"Unless she didn't end it all?" Iris questioned, Coral completely unaware that she'd moved and was now standing on the other side of the room looking at some of the flower arrangements.

"What do you mean?" Daniella asked.

"Maybe Camilla wasn't the cause of her own life having been taken away... maybe someone else was," Iris said, turning around to lock eyes with Daniella. Coral understood: she was trying to play bad cop and ease it out of her that way, but that would only work if she knew anything, of course.

Daniella didn't even flinch. "But why would anyone do that?" she asked.

"Who knows," Iris said, slowly walking back towards the counter, "maybe someone was jealous of her loving family, caring husband, and thriving business? Maybe they wanted that for themselves and thought they'd take it from her?"

Daniella still didn't alter her expression. *This woman's poker face is very impressive,* Coral thought. *Or does she really have no idea what we're talking about?*

"I can't imagine her having a grievance with anyone; literally everyone I knew only had good to say about her. It was just so sad," Daniella said, looking down at the photo and then back up at Coral. "If you would like the photo to keep, you can take it. It's of no use to me, but I know she'd have wanted you to have a piece of her from her past. It was around this time of year, all those years ago, in which she found her true love and passion for flowers; summer was always her favourite season."

Coral held the photo frame in her hands. "Who is the man in the photo?"

"That's Gary, who owned the shop when that photo was taken. He took a shine to your mum; he thought she did amazing things with flowers, and she even won us a few awards with her green fingers..."

"What about you? Did he take a shine to you?" Iris asked, going in for the kill yet again.

"For a while, yes, but Cammy created the most amazing arrangements, there was no doubt about that. Nothing could overtake what she designed."

"So, where is the owner of the shop now? Is he still around here?" Coral asked, her voice laced with hope. If he took such a shine to her mum, maybe he could shed some light too on the mystery at hand.

"You're talking to her right now." Daniella smiled proudly, but she still looked exhausted. "Once Cammy moved on and became self-employed, business plummeted, and the passion was gone from Gary's eyes. He wanted to sell up, but I needed this job, so I took it on by myself. Business isn't what it used to be, but it pays the bills. There'll come a day when the flowers die along with my hope for this place, but for now, I'm keeping it going on what little energy I still possess. It's just a shame. It was the most popular place to get flowers back in its heyday." Daniella hopped off the stool and pushed it back under. "Anyway, would you still like your flower arrangement?"

Coral felt disheartened. This woman really did believe in her mum and that she was a beautiful soul that had sadly left this world, but something didn't sit right. Probably because she didn't get the answer she expected, but she couldn't give up hope now; she had to see this thought process through.

****

Once Coral and Iris were back in the truck, they sat for a little while staring out of the window.

"You seem sad," Iris commented. "You didn't get the answers you thought you'd hear, did you?"

Coral shook her head.

"It's not that… it's just, she knew mum wouldn't have had a reason to kill herself but didn't believe anyone would have a reason to kill her either… It was just a bit of a deflating conversation with no new information in sight."

"Maybe she was just stunned by what you'd asked her? I mean, she's probably never met you, or at least hasn't seen you since you were small, and she didn't have any reason to talk about your mum for years either; she could still find it hard for all we know." Coral nodded and looked out of the window in front of her. "They were probably close once; she could've found it a struggle seeing you and talking about her again; old wounds being picked apart to feel like fresh ones again sort of thing," Iris said.

"I'm not sure," Coral murmured. "Shall I go back in and give her my number in case she thinks of anything else she might want to tell me?"

As Coral decided she would give her number to Daniella, not waiting for Iris's response, she turned to get back out of the truck when she noticed the closed sign was up in the florist's door window and that the lights that were moments ago illuminating the flower shop had now gone out; the shop coated in complete darkness.

10

Coral waited a few moments before she got out of the truck. Staring up at the grand stone house before her, which had three floors and was a hell of a lot more grand than her own, she felt shivers go down her spine. As beautiful as the house was, she knew inside it only held coldness, similar to her own home.

"Sums up my family," she murmured to herself before turning around and poking her head through the truck window. "Any chance you can pretend to be me and go in?"

Iris smiled and batted her eyelashes. "If I was blessed with snow-white skin and coral-pink hair, you know I would, but unfortunately, that's all you. You'll be fine, just... don't break anything," she said and pulled an amused grimace which made Coral let out a shaky laugh, sparking up memories of the past family arguments, which swiftly turned into fights and being threatened to replace many priceless antiques. None of them managed to get replaced in the long run.

Turning around with as much enthusiasm as she could muster, Coral began to ascend the stone steps, each one feeling like the size of a mountain to climb up. She couldn't even remember the last time she had visited her Aunt Eva, but then again, when was the last time she'd been invited around? Kruze definitely would've been invited, or at least blessed with a phone call to see how his life was, but then again, he'd never been threatened with a restraining order like she had. Coral always resented the fact her Aunt Eva didn't really like her, always picking faults and never praising her for things she did achieve, even if the list wasn't that long. Was she jealous of the fact that she had never been blessed with a daughter? Or ashamed because the girl Coral had become wasn't your average eighteen-year-old and acted in the complete opposite way to how she would've brought her up? The possibilities were endless as to why.

Reaching the top of the steps, Coral pressed a finger against the doorbell, watching through the stained glass in the door for any signs of movement. As she listened to the tinny tune, she noticed how the doorbell had a few blemishes. Just as Coral began to question this, the door slowly opened, revealing a woman who most definitely didn't look like the Aunt Eva she remembered. All traces of the woman with beautiful prim and proper features and just all-out elegance had gone. Stood before her was a replica, but with untamed hair, deep black circles around her eyes and a lounge set hanging from her still curvaceous body. That was one of the only physical differences between her mum and Aunt Eva: her mum was slim and lacking curves, whereas Aunt Eva made up for that; however, her slightly towering height disguised any extra weight she carried. Her wine-stained lips parted, and a snarl started to form.

"Coral… it's three o'clock in the afternoon…" Aunt Eva said, swishing her wine glass as she spoke.

"I wasn't aware you knew what time of day it was," Coral responded, nodding at the wine glass. "I need to speak to you, please."

Aunt Eva let out a low chuckle and leant against the door frame. "And why would *you* want to talk to *me*?

Why don't you talk to... oh wait, no you can't, he never leaves his room, does he," Aunt Eva chortled, taking a sip of her drink. Without warning, something seemed to spark in her aunt's mind, and so she stood up straighter, swaying slightly and stepping to the side. "Just come in, will you? I don't want the neighbours seeing you here."

Coral stepped forward over the threshold and slipped off her boots. Aunt Eva sauntered through to the living room, her manicured feet padding against the cold white marble floor, Coral following behind, taking in the environment around her. Everything was exactly how it was before: perfect, or near enough at least, but that was her thought process before she got into the living room, which looked the most lived in. Piles of magazines, bowls of nuts, and at least three empty bottles of red wine scattered across the glass coffee table suggested her aunt was going through a crisis, whether it be midlife or just in general.

Aunt Eva parked herself down on the sofa, spilling a few drops of wine as she did, muttering to herself and shovelled a handful of nuts into her mouth, crunching away as if Coral wasn't present at all. Coral carefully sat herself down in the armchair opposite, eyeing up the state of the room, not being able to place this with the Aunt Eva she once knew. But then again, years had passed by, times had changed, and she had let herself go; they both had. "Why are you here? You never visit, you never call—"

"Aunt Eva, you don't even like me, so why would I do those things and waste my breath?" Coral commented.

"Well, you're doing it now, aren't you?" she asked, taking a long sip of her wine and draining the glass completely.

Coral sighed and rolled her eyes. This was going to be a tough conversation, one she wished so badly she didn't have to have. Aunt Eva was just impossible to communicate with, and as she stood up to go get herself some more wine, taking her empty wine glass with her, Coral suddenly realised what she could smell. She wasn't ashamed that she recognised the smell instantly; she was more stunned that Aunt Eva would tolerate it, especially after she'd been scolded by her before for smoking it, let alone in this house.

Aunt Eva entered the room again and sat herself back down, placing a half-empty bottle of red wine on the table, her wine glass swishing around with what had been the rest of the bottle's contents.

"Since when did you tolerate weed?" Coral asked, her eyebrows knitting together in confusion, feeling slightly smug without letting it show.

"Since when did you question your elders?" she fired back.

"Haven't I always?"

Aunt Eva took a polite sip from her wine glass. "You are most definitely a very *distinctive* individual, Coral. Now, can you please get on with your questions? What is it for, a school quiz or something?"

"Well—" Coral started, but then thought to herself, maybe asking the questions on behalf of something to do with sixth form could be a better way to get answers from her. If Aunt Eva thought it was education-related and not just her delving into the dreary past of their family affairs, maybe she'd open up a bit more. "Yes, I'm doing psychology, and we have to ask particular questions to see how individuals' minds work and how their answers vary from our own."

"And you wanted *me* to answer them? Why?" she questioned.

"You're interesting and opinionated beyond belief, especially in comparison to my mindset, so I thought your answers would be best to hear as they would be completely opposite to what I would answer with," Coral replied.

Aunt Eva scoffed. "Like you've ever wanted to hear what I've had to say in years gone by. Fine," Aunt Eva said, this time taking a longer sip of her drink, "go ahead, but don't take up too much of my time. I've got important matters to attend to."

"I'm sure you do," Coral replied, and with that she got a stern look from her aunt. She pulled out her phone as if to show she was reading questions. "Question one: do you have regrets in life?"

"Yes, I do," Aunt Eva slurred.

"Can you elaborate?"

"I regret most of my life, if not all of it, including letting you into my house a few moments ago and wasting precious moments of the time I have left on this earth."

Coral was taken aback by this, obviously not the part about herself but about Aunt Eva regretting most of her life. Aunt Eva had always looked so proud of her achievements and everything she had been blessed with in life. How could she regret it all?

"Okay... question two: do you have any grudges you still hold?"

"Most definitely," Aunt Eva said, no hint of sarcasm.

"Really? How can a woman such as yourself have regrets and hold grudges?" Coral asked, a slight twinge of anger prickling within her. "You have *everything* you've ever wanted: the perfect family, the perfect job, the perfect house. You have it all, and yet, this is how you feel?" Coral questioned, heat slowly rising up her neck.

She was getting angry and frustrated now and didn't want to, but with Aunt Eva, she always had to make any situation about herself, even when nothing was truly wrong. Being sprayed with the wrong shade of fake tan would be worse than people starving from malnutrition in her aunt's eyes. *I won't break anything; I won't break anything,* Coral thought to herself, chanting it in her mind and trying her best to find the truth behind it.

Aunt Eva turned her attention away from her wine glass and stared at Coral with a spaced-out look on her face. "You think my life is *perfect*?"

"Yes? Obviously, it is. You've got everything you've ever wanted, and yet it still isn't enough for you, is it?" Coral's hands began to shake, so she buried them in her lap, squeezing them tight. She refused to show that Aunt Eva was getting to her on an emotional level.

"You think I've got *everything* I've ever wanted, Coral?"

"Yes I do, actually."

"You think yourself to be so knowledgeable, Coral, and yet, you are only 18. You know *nothing*. No one has everything they ever want in life. Not even me," she said, placing her glass down on the coffee table.

"Really? And what is it you don't have? Because you look to me like you've got everything you could ever want." Coral opened her arms out to indicate the room they were in and how grand and exquisite it was, just like the rest of the house. "People like me can only dream of the luxuries you have and the amazing future you certified for yourself." Coral looked away and down to the floor. *Focus yourself*, she thought, *don't let her tip you over the edge.*

"My future isn't amazing, and it never will be."

"Well, you have a funny way of looking at it," Coral muttered and then suddenly stopped as the sound of glass shattering filled her ears and made her body shake from the inside out, her hands flying up to her head to protect herself.

Daringly, she raised her gaze to the coffee table. The half-empty glass of red wine was gone, and when she looked to her left, she realised it had been launched across the room, and now, on the beautiful lace patterned white wall, red streaks seeped downwards, as if someone had just been shot in front of it and a blood bath explosion now dripped down the wall. Her eyes then met her Aunt Eva's, and Coral noticed something feral shone in her bloodshot eyes.

"How *dare* you," Aunt Eva spat. "You're so much like your mother it's unbelievable. All I see in you is *her*. All I see when I look at you is a selfish brat with no care for anyone else and their feelings—"

"Don't you *dare* talk about my mum that way" Coral interrupted. "She was a *good, loyal* person." Coral was raising her voice now, but she didn't care; she wasn't about to sit here and watch this crazed woman talk rubbish about her mum that way.

Aunt Eva let out somewhat of a cackle and snatched out for the wine bottle as if someone might take it from her, then pointed the open end at Coral, causing her to flinch in case she lost her grip on it.

"*Good* and *loyal?* Don't jest with me, girl. That *mother* of yours was never good and loyal to *me*. She was *selfish* and *cruel* and has been ever since the day she was birthed into this world."

"What are you talking about? You can't just slate her now she's dead," Coral snapped back, tears starting to form in her eyes, stinging them and making her squeeze them shut. For just one moment, in that total darkness formed by closing her eyes, she felt better and at peace. Aunt Eva would always be at the top of her list of the people she most hated in this world, without a doubt. They would never find compromise between each other, whether that was a good thing or a bad thing, she didn't know.

"Oh, I slated her long before that, dear child, especially once she hit the grand old age of 16 and ruined my chances at a better life," Aunt Eva said, examining her nails, her long slender fingers extended.

"What do you mean?"

Aunt Eva completely ignored her and continued to rant. "Please, Coral, never, and I mean *never*, ruin someone else's chance at happiness. It's sinful and—"

"Just tell me what you *fucking* mean, Eva," Coral shouted, the tears racing down her face in an attempt to soak her skin through. "If you want to be the adult here, then speak up instead of just rattling on with the same shit you always dish out. Give me a valid reason as to why she was such a bad person in your eyes."

Aunt Eva stood up slowly, taking a deep breath, smoothing her hair and clothes down in an attempt to gain composure and dominance. "I was 18 and your mother was 16. She got a newfound confidence in herself once certain aspects of her body had become *bigger* and *firmer* and more noticeable to those around her, so she used it to her advantage. Your father was 21 when he finally decided to host a party at his family home. Obviously, back then, he was an extremely popular guy, and all the girls wanted him, including me. And he had *always* asked to dance with me at house parties and dances in the village, and I knew this would be the time he would ask me to be *his* one and only. It was on the cards, everyone talked of it... that's when my mother, your grandma, *ruined* everything; and Camilla, my sister, *your* damned mother... I despise them both to this day for what they did..." Aunt Eva paced back and forth in front of Coral, not once giving eye contact. Coral preferred it that way; the less she had to look into her Aunt Eva's bloodshot angry eyes, the better.

"Okay..." Coral said as Aunt Eva continued pacing in front of her with determination, leaving solid silence hanging in the air. Not one glance was given to the wine-stained wall. *Out of character for Aunt Eva on exasperating levels,* Coral thought; she was an extremely tidy person, but in an obsessive way, and loved living up to a showroom standard with her home.

"So, I was ready for the party of the year," Aunt Eva continued, "the night where my life would change forever, when my mother told me I had to take Camilla with me. You can imagine I wasn't too keen on the idea; after all, this was going to be *my* special night. But after much disagreement, I went along with it. I was in too much of a good mood to let it ruin my evening, an evening I had waited a long time for. If only I'd known... if only I'd known what *she* was going to do..."

"Who?"

Aunt Eva scoffed. "Your selfish *mother*; that's who. Camilla got dressed up in some horrifyingly short skirt and a velvet long-sleeved top she had cut so it just hung below where her bra should've been. It was so distasteful and left nothing to the imagination. I was mortified just having to bring her with me and have her be an accessory to me. Not like I went around the party with her; I left her to her own devices. But I felt so beautiful walking up the steps to the house that night, in my royal blue sequin dress, picturing myself taking those steps when Jayden and I were boyfriend and girlfriend one day, hand in hand. I'd bought it especially as I knew your father loved that colour. But then... goodness, the memory gets me so *angry*. I didn't want Camilla there because I knew she'd get tangled up in some trouble that wasn't hers to get tangled up in and that I'd have to answer for it when we got home to mother..."

"What trouble did she get tangled up in?"

Aunt Eva stopped and took a sharp breath, not giving Coral a glance, as if she were replaying the memory in her mind and feeling the pain of it as if it were happening now. As if she could feel everything she felt before.

"I couldn't find Jayden anywhere. I looked everywhere for him, and I gathered he was just lost among the crowd of people in his living room dancing around or getting more bottles from the cellar. So I went up to the bathroom to freshen up... and that's when I heard *noises* coming from his parents' bedroom... So I opened the door and found... and found..."

"What did you find?" Coral asked, but she had a feeling she already knew.

"I found your mother tangled up in trouble. *My* trouble. *My* chance at happiness. *My* future."

Coral sat dumbfounded. No wonder Aunt Eva had always acted the way she had towards her. It was obvious now, but she just couldn't believe that her dad and Aunt Eva had ever had a thing going on. Clearly it wasn't much of a thing if he chose her mum so quickly.

"She toyed with his heart with her short skirts and braless chest; she practically threw herself at him. I was waiting until I was married like any good Christian girl should do. Your mother clearly had other ideas and went against everything Christian girls go to church and learn about. God should've struck her down with lightning when he had the chance and your father also."

Aunt Eva raised the bottle to her mouth and took a long hard drink, so much that Coral thought she was going to finish it all in one go.

"Did my dad ever explain himself to you once he realised who he'd slept with?"

"He never mentioned anything to me, no apology for the way he just strung me along for months on end, no concern was shown whatsoever towards me and my feelings. I was merely a distraction, a chess piece in the game he was playing, the appetizer to the main course that my sister clearly was when she walked into his life, or more like humped into his life. He was practically dating a child and didn't even care, but no one seemed to throw hate their way, not even my own mother; she never once objected, she was just happy Camilla was with a decent man. The decent man *I* should've been with, but then he got her pregnant, so he didn't have a choice but to care for her and stick around."

"When did they marry?"

"Once Camilla was 18, of course, but she'd already had Kruze by this point and then you. Perfect home, perfect family, perfect job. Perfect everything. Selfish to kill herself, really," Aunt Eva went on to say, scoffing.

She's drunk and jealous, Coral thought. *Breathe through the anger you feel; she's not in a sane state of mind with what she's saying.*

"And you believe she killed herself?" Coral asked, the anger coursing through her veins trying its best to take over, but she knew she couldn't let it if she wanted to get the answers she'd come here to listen to and endure.

Aunt Eva's face changed slightly, only ever so slightly, but not enough for Coral to clearly see what the change of expression meant. Nothing was said for a good few seconds, but it didn't take long before Aunt Eva took a deep, steady breath and then exhaled.

"You believe someone killed her," she quietly acknowledged, her voice full of exhaustion. The fight in her was wilting away like the flowers in the almost empty vase in the living room window.

"I don't believe a woman who had the world could just leave it behind so easily, as everyone says she did," Coral carefully stated, giving her aunt eye contact the entire time.

"Then who do you believe could kill her?"

"I was hoping you could answer that question."

Just as Aunt Eva was about to answer, both their ears pricked up as loud footsteps were sounded, which then revealed a very lanky looking teenager with scruffy blonde hair and big headphones on entering the room. He rolled his eyes at the scene before him, then did a double-take as he noticed Coral.

"Coral... Wow, I didn't expect to see you... *here,*" he said, his voice a lot deeper than she last remembered. Then again, the last time she'd seen her cousin Darren he was but a child. "How've you—"

"I didn't know you were still here, Darren," Aunt Eva said, cutting her son off from conversing with Coral. Once again, Aunt Eva attempted to smooth out her hair and clothes, wiping away wine that had missed her mouth and had stained her chin in the process.

"I came back not long ago to get a few things I forgot. Is everything okay?" he asked, signalling towards Coral and then staring at the tarnished white wall with wide brown eyes.

"Fine, darling, everything's fine," she said, fluttering her hands and showing a cringe-worthy attempt at a smile.

"Well, that's clearly a slight exaggeration, isn't it," he said, walking over to pick up the broken wine glass, then dropped it back down effortlessly, clearly realising it was too messy of a job for him to attempt.

"Anyway," he continued, "I hope you're well, Coral. We should go for a walk sometime and have a catch up; it feels like forever since we last saw each other," he said, sauntering back towards the archway of the living room. "Right, Mum, I'm off to Dad's, so I'll see you on Monday night." With that, he was gone as fast as he'd appeared.

Coral sat astounded once again, not understanding how the perfect life her aunt had made out to have, had slowly crumbled away to dust, and she'd had no idea about it. With hesitation, she slowly moved her eyes to look at her Aunt Eva's, but she was looking away, tears forming, biting her lip which looked like a day-to-day habit for her with the deep indentations in her bottom lip.

This wasn't the Aunt Eva she had grown up knowing; this woman before her was completely in tatters, hardly a trace left of her original self. She was exhausted with life, and Coral could clearly see that. Once again, she hadn't got the answers she was searching for and wanted about her mum and her death, but she was done with the torment between her and her aunt and was ready to let her go on with her life without any more delving. Enough had been learnt today to last her a lifetime, and for once, her heart was telling her to not put her aunt through any more grief, no matter how cruel she'd been to her throughout her life. Aunt Eva had her reasons, and even though Coral hadn't had a chance to process them yet, she knew she had to be the bigger person if her aunt couldn't be.

Standing up on shaky legs, she cleared her throat and looked at her aunt. "I'll go now, Aunt Eva. I'm sorry that things took this turn between us, and I'm sorry you despise me. I know you struggle to get on with me and accept me because of... my mum... and what happened between you both, but I'm Coral Bayles; I'm not Camilla Bayles."

As Coral made her way to the front door, sliding on her boots as quickly as possible, she carefully stepped over the threshold once more and closed the stained-glass door behind her until she heard it click shut. Then, all that was left in the grand home were the loud sobs reverberating off the walls of a woman who had lost everything.

11

"I'm just on my way to Dylan's," Coral lied down the phone to Iris, trying her best to sound as perky as possible, but the nerves were beginning to take over. She stared out of the top deck bus window absentmindedly at the unfamiliar surroundings in absolute awe, yet a slither of anxiousness was slowly creeping up her spine.

"I don't know why you tolerate that idiot," Iris said into Coral's ear through the phone, crackling sounds making their way through in unison as she got further into the countryside.

"Me neither sometimes," Coral sighed. "I'll be fine, though; he'll be normal once I've buttered him up and batted my eyelashes, then I can ask him my questions. He can't complain that I've not paid him any attention either; I've been a busy girl, and he has to remember that. The world doesn't revolve around him," Coral said, a sad feeling washing over her. "Anyway, I'll call or message when I can."

As Coral hung up and put her phone back in her pocket, she felt a sudden pang of guilt, but then a shiver ran down her spine, and she remembered *why* she was doing what she was doing, but the cold feeling remained as if someone had just poured ice down her back as a reminder. The guilt was from both lying to Iris *and* not making any time for Dylan recently. But then again, he wasn't exactly a top priority right now, just as she wasn't to him unless he needed the appetite in his pants fulfilling. She was still angry about the pocketing of the horrific coloured knickers situation, but she would deal with that later; there were more important things going on in her world right now.

The bus began to slow down, and Coral's stomach turned and twisted, making her almost want to throw up, but she swallowed it back down and began her descent down the steps and out onto the quiet country road, taking in the view and the balmy morning weather before her. A line of cottages on the opposite side of the road, a diner and a few shops further down were all her eyes allowed her to see from where she stood, and suddenly, she felt scared and *very* alone. *I shouldn't have come out here on my own*, Coral thought, looking around, but nothing familiarised itself with her.

She was as far from Dylan's flat as she was from her own home. It hadn't taken her long to find the bus that would get her to the next village over from hers, but it didn't make her feel any more confident about the situation. For all she knew, the person she was about to come face to face with could be the reason her mum took her own life, or even the hands behind her life being taken away. This stranger was most likely her last hope of finally bolting shut the door on the past that haunted her so much.

Coral knew deep down she shouldn't be doing any of this, asking questions about how her mum died, raking the past back up, re-opening old wounds. This was a job Kruze should've been doing or what another police officer should've done all those years ago, but to Coral, none of the past was set in stone, and she was almost completely losing belief in what she had been told had happened to her mum.

According to those around her, Coral's mum had been a free spirit who enjoyed every aspect of life. If she'd shown signs of sadness or depression, then she would've surely confided in her husband, maybe even Aunt Eva at a push, or somebody who was willing to listen to her; anyone would've made time for her, just as she did for everyone else. However, that was the thing; there were no signs whatsoever. No one Coral had spoken to had noticed anything to make them think twice about the state of her mum's mental health, as if there were no despairing thoughts in her mum's head at all; they all had the same positive answer to give. Her mum had been the type of woman to fight against any waves of negativity that ever tried to hit her in life; she weathered any storm. Unlike Coral, who tried her best to battle against the rough water, but constantly felt like she was drowning, as the waves of depression hit her at full force over and over again like they had done for years.

Coral shook her head, trying her best to dislodge any of the saddening thoughts that were doing laps around her mind, and began scanning the row of cottages before her. She lightly jogged over the quiet road in front of her, focusing her attention on number three, and made haste through the mint green wooden gate and along the crazy paving pathway on unsteady legs. Where was the strong, fearless lioness she knew she was deep down, and why had she been replaced with this anxiety-ridden little mouse?

Coral rang the doorbell and patiently waited. Nothing happened. She rang it again and knocked on the door, but once again, there was no sign of movement through the glass in the door to indicate that anyone had heard her.

Without warning, she heard someone clear their throat behind her. Coral spun around and saw, peeping over one of the hedges in the garden, two beady dark eyes looking back at her.

"Who are you, and what are you doing on this private property?" a croaky well-spoken voice asked, the eyes of the hidden person not once blinking or leaving Coral's, completely transfixed.

"Sorry—"

"Are you a relative or a friend of the owner of this property?"

"Can I at least see who I'm talking to, please?" Coral asked, holding her hand above her eyes to shield them from the morning sun.

A stout little woman with more liver spots than Coral could count appeared from behind the hedge, a mustard-coloured dress and floral apron wrapped so tightly around her that you could see the material was thinning out by an extreme amount, and the gaps between the buttons were gaping from being pulled so taut; definitely not the most flattering of outfit choices she could've chosen for herself. She had a look of an old-fashioned pot doll, except her cheeks were extra rouged and her hair a mass of frizzy autumnal colours on her head, looking in great need of an extreme wash and comb through.

"Now you've seen me, I will ask you again: are you a relative or a friend of the owner of this property?"

Coral leant on one leg and then swapped and put her weight on the other; she felt beyond awkward from how this little woman was speaking to her. "Well, not quite either, but—"

"Well then, take your monstrous hair and the rest of you off this private property before I call the police for trespassing. He's been through enough this year. He doesn't need idiots like you disrupting him even more," she said, pointing a soil-ridden hand at her.

"But I—"

"I said move it, you clown, before I ring the police." The small, stout woman, who resembled the look of a pot doll to Coral, placed her dirty hands on her hips and furrowed her eyebrows so hard, Coral thought they were going to crack her skin as if she were as delicate as porcelain; obviously her face, not her soul, which seemed cracked beyond repair showing through her rudeness towards Coral.

Coral didn't hesitate and walked swiftly down the path and out through the gateway. Beginning her walk along the road, she trudged past the cottage next door, where a sun-kissed woman leant over the stone wall and gave her a cheery grin. Two small children were playing in her front garden, and they all seemed a lot friendlier than the ignorant pot doll she'd just spoken to.

"Are you alright, love?" she asked with a thick country accent. Coral smiled wearily at the woman and edged herself closer to the stone wall. "Don't worry about her; she's always got a bee in her bonnet. Are you looking for Rodney?"

Coral nodded. "Yes, I am, but if he's not wanting visitors—"

"Oh, Rodney loves a good natter, I'll tell you. If you keep walking down the road, you'll see a place called Wallflower Diner. He should be in there; he goes every Sunday morning for breakfast," she said, smiling at Coral, the children behind her now waving and smiling at her. "He says he goes for the coffee, but we all know he loves those scrambled eggs on toast the most," she said and winked.

"Thank you so much," Coral said, a hint of gratitude laced within her words as she began to make her way down the road towards what she hoped would be the last stretch of this mystery maze she felt stranded in.

You can still go home, right now, no questions asked, she thought to herself, but she had to do this for her mum's sake as well as her own. If anyone was going to get answers about what had happened to her mum and potentially have the chance to clarify if it was suicide or if there was more than meets the eye in this horror story of her life, then it was going to be Coral.

The diner looked more like a mobile home on the outside, except for it clearly having a permanent residence in the spot it was in. *This is it*, Coral thought, her legs feeling like jelly. As she ascended the stairs and slowly opened the door, a bell rang above her head, causing her to jump and scrunch her eyes tightly shut. Her heart was pounding in her chest, her hands twitching as she stepped into the diner and felt the gentle change of the temperature on her skin, causing goosebumps to rise up.

Taking steady deep breaths to try and control her heart from going into overdrive, she let the door close behind her and looked around at her surroundings. There were at least 10 tables and chairs, each with a small bunch of flowers in a vase in the centre. The flowers looked as if they were standing tall and proud, each bunch ready and waiting to be looked at in awe of how beautiful they were by the potential customers. Coral slowly walked down the centre of the diner and passed the few people having their breakfast; she arrived at the counter, gazing at the assortment of pastries and cakes in the glass cabinet, imagining just how sweet and scrumptious they would taste in her mouth.

A slender middle-aged woman with jet black hair and glossy red lipstick appeared from behind the counter, making Coral once again become startled. "Are you alright, sweetheart? Sorry if I gave you a fright; I was just getting out more napkins. What can I get you?" she asked, chewing her gum which made her face look wrinklier with each chew.

"Well, I'm... looking for someone who apparently comes here for breakfast every Sunday," Coral said, fiddling with her watch strap; she felt ridiculous. "I was told he might be here?"

"Who is it you're looking for, sweetie?"

"His name is Rodney... I'm unsure of his last—"

"You're looking for me?" a man asked to her left in the corner by the window, moving the newspaper he was reading to reveal a pure white moustache and wiry beard fixed upon his face; confusion etching at his features. His eyebrows furrowed once he took in Coral's complexion, clearly not recognising the stranger before him. "Do I know you?"

"No, you don't... You don't know me as such, but... I think you knew my... my..." Coral's words trailed off, and she looked down at the floor. She felt beyond awkward doing this; these people didn't know who she was and all she wanted to do was go home, curl up in a ball under her duvet and fall apart. "I'm sorry," she said and turned to go.

"Wait." The elderly man, who Coral guessed was Rodney, stood up, pushing his chair back suddenly, holding the table edge to steady himself. "You said you thought I knew someone. Who did you think I knew?"

Coral slowly turned back and locked eyes with Rodney. He looked kind, but that didn't mean he wouldn't have hurt her mum or given her a reason to hurt herself. "I thought you knew my mum... she was your gardener years ago, I think—"

"Camilla is your mother? Well, I'll be damned. Please, come take a seat with me," he said and gestured to the table, taking his seat once more, a joyful yet surprised look spreading across his face. "Jenny, please set this young lady up with your finest mug of coffee. It's the least I can do."

"I'll get right on it," the woman behind the counter said, turning around and seeing to it right away. Coral took a few shaky steps towards the table and perched on the chair in front of her, readying herself for if she needed to flee.

Rodney took a sip of his coffee and cupped his hands around the mug. Coral noticed the cracked skin thinning as he gripped the mug tighter, so much she thought it was going to tear. The way he looked at Coral was in true admiration, no hint of unkindness in his weather-worn skin. "So, is it true you're Camilla's daughter?" he asked with eagerness laced within his voice.

Coral nodded. "Yes, I'm Coral. Are you Rodney, the man she gardened for?"

"Yes, I am indeed, but I can assure you, I highly doubt there was only me that she gardened for. Your mother is an astounding gardener, and I was saddened when she never got back in touch to come and garden for me again. I just assumed she had a busy life with her family and wanted time with you all. She was a damn sight better than my current gardener Maureen; she can't half be a pain," he said and then chuckled to himself.

"Yeah, I went to your house to find you and bumped into her... Not the most polite of women I've come across," Coral said, smiling slightly.

"You've got that right. Oh, do tell me, how is your mother keeping? Is she well?" Rodney asked, eyes glistening with happiness.

Coral flinched at the question as if she had just been prodded with a red-hot poker. Was this to throw her off of the trail, or was it a genuine concerned question? How could she even answer that? "Hold on... you really don't know?" she asked him. Rodney's face was slowly losing its enthusiastic look, and confusion spread across his face like the first rays of sun in the morning.

"What is it I'm supposed to know?" he asked, a smile still set in place, clearly just being a polite gentleman.

Coral looked up as Jenny placed a piping hot mug of coffee in front of her. She smiled and nodded in thanks, then looked down into the mug. "My mum died, Rodney... She died five years ago."

"What?" he gasped, and his face quickly crumpled. He looked ever so sad, and a few tears spilled over his leather-like skin within seconds of hearing the words leave her mouth. "I... I wasn't aware... I just thought... My goodness, young lady, I am so terribly sorry," he said, reaching forward to hold Coral's hands. They were warm in hers and brought her comfort, which helped to reduce the fear she had felt from the moment of stepping foot into the diner. "I wish I'd have known. I would've attended the funeral and sent flowers as a mark of respect. Please tell me, how did she die? Was it childbirth, an accident, an illness?" he asked, searching her face for answers.

"Well, that's why I came to see you," she said, leaning back into her seat, letting her hands fall from Rodney's, and taking a sip of her coffee completely oblivious to the burning sensation on her tongue. "She was found at the lake near my home... her wrists slit, face down in the lake... suicide *apparently*," she said, looking out of the window at the sheep in the field next to the diner. *What it would be like to be a sheep, happy, carefree, munching on grass all day*, Coral thought enviously. The pain in her chest felt too sickening for her to speak; every time she spoke of her mum's death, a small part of her died inside.

"I don't believe that for a second, not a chance would your mother have killed herself... she loved life, she loved her job, and she loved her family. She had no reason I was aware of to end her life... I'm flabbergasted," Rodney said, shaking his head and rubbing his face with his hands, looking well and truly deflated. "You've shocked me to the core, Coral, you truly have. Your mother was like the daughter I never had. She made both my late wife and I so happy. We loved what your mother did with our gardens; it was truly the most beautiful scene to witness outside our home."

Rodney pulled a handkerchief out from his pocket and dabbed his eyes. "Camilla cared so deeply for her job, throwing so much passion into it. She was a beautiful flower in this world; I used to say that to her every time she came to my home," he said and gave a sad smile from remembering the treasured time in the past. "I'm so disheartened to hear she is no longer in this world of ours, and I'm finding it most upsetting to only be learning of this now when so much time has passed. How could I have been so naïve to think she would just stop all contact with me after the strong friendship we had built?"

Coral felt stunned by the response Rodney showed. He was a sad old man, who hadn't just lost his wife, but Coral's own mother also; she clearly meant so much to him and had left a lasting impression on him like a daughter would. You could see that in his face and how much it hurt hearing of the loss of her. Hearing him speak of her mother with such kind words painted a beautiful picture of the woman she wished was still here.

"She was really something, wasn't she," Coral said, smiling to herself, a few tears making their way down her face, the emotions too strong to hold in this time.

"Yes," Rodney said, a smile starting to spread across his face again while a few tears of his own flowed, "she really was; such a sad loss to this world. You should be proud to have had a mother like her; you definitely take after her with looks. Maybe not the hair, but I can imagine she would've loved the colour."

This made Coral's eyes fill up even more, but this time, she decided to let a few more tears shed instead of holding them back. *I hope so*, she thought, running her fingers through her hair.

* * * *

After much conversation about her mum, talking to Rodney about Kruze and her dad, and hearing about Rodney's late wife, she sat back in her chair and sighed;

the relief from talking to this wonderful man was like removing a tight grip from around her neck, the suffocating feeling had been held at bay for now. She knew for a fact this man had loved and respected her mum just as much as she had, and it confirmed to her even more that her mum couldn't have ended her own life; she couldn't have had a reason to.

* * * *

Rodney and Coral finished their mugs of coffee and smiled at one another.

"Well, looks like it's time for me to get home. Would you like to join me for some tea and biscuits? I could get us set up in the garden if you'd like," Rodney suggested, standing up and pushing his chair underneath the table, Coral following suit.

"Thank you, but I should be getting back home. I've no idea when the next bus will be, so I should really get myself sorted; I've got important stuff to do," Coral replied, smiling bashfully.

"Quite alright," Rodney said, picking up his walking stick and gesturing towards the door, "I'll walk you back to the bus stop at least."

Rodney turned and looked over towards where Jenny was by the counter. "Thank you again, Jenny; always a beautiful Sunday morning." Jenny gave them both a smile as she headed for their table and started to clean up.

The bell above the door sounded above their heads, but this time, Coral relaxed at the sound, all fear gone from within. *I wonder if mum ever came here to this diner*, Coral thought, smiling as the mid-morning sunshine hit her skin, reminding her of the time of day.

Coral and Rodney walked along the pavement, enjoying each other's company and the quiet of their surroundings. Feeling totally at ease compared to before, Coral felt so much lighter in comparison. She thought this place was beautiful; no wonder her mum chose to work out here. There was just one thing that sprung to her mind that made her anxiousness start to creep up on her, but she knew if she asked, Rodney would happily put her at ease, just as he had done all morning in the time they'd spent in the diner.

"Well," Coral said as they arrived outside Rodney's home opposite the bus stop, checking her phone for the update, "looks like my bus won't be for another five minutes, so that was good timing."

"Indeed so," Rodney replied. "The bus stop you need is just a few paces along the road so you best be getting a move on if you want to make it," he said, smiling and gesturing with his walking stick. "I really enjoyed your company this morning."

"The feeling is mutual... but before I go," Coral started, "earlier on, you asked how my mum had died. What were the reasons you thought again? You listed them to me. I just can't quite remember," Coral asked, not letting the anxiety take over, keeping it at bay as best she could. She'd made plenty of progress this morning and wasn't going to let that be ruined.

"Oh goodness, my mind isn't what it used to be. Let me think... I asked about illness... accident and... and..." Rodney stroked his beard with his free hand, his eyebrows knitting together. "Ah yes, I remember: childbirth."

Coral let out a gentle, steady laugh. "Well, it definitely wouldn't have been childbirth; Kruze and

I were a handful without the idea of a third child being brought into this world."

"Oh, well, I only suggested that as she was with child when I last saw her," he said, once again a solemn look appearing on his face.

Coral's smile faltered, and it felt as though her heart had missed a beat, a sick feeling twisting and turning within her like a ship on rocky waters and adding to it a prickly hot sensation in the pit of her stomach, making her want to jump overboard from what she'd just heard.

"That can't be right... she always said she just wanted two children, and that's what she was blessed with... there's no way..."

"No, no, I may say my mind isn't what it used to be, Coral, but I know for a fact she was with child when I last saw her. She spoke in confidence about it, though, to both my late wife and I," Rodney said, leaning against the stone wall behind him, catching his breath best he could, the heat clearly taking its toll on him.

"Spoke to you in confidence? Why would she have needed to do that?" Coral asked, and as she waited for an answer, she felt the first trickle of sweat slide down her back. This wasn't what she had expected to hear. *There must be some mistake,* she thought.

"Oh yes, in confidence. She needed advice, and therefore my late wife and I tried to advise her the best we could. She was in desperation, you see," he said.

"Desperation? Why?" Coral asked, the back of her neck getting clammy and her breath quickening. Rodney looked sorrowful and lost all colour in his face. This *really* couldn't be good.

"I'm sorry to be the one to tell you this... especially under the circumstances, but the baby wasn't planned for. It was an act of sexual assault by a man she didn't intend to get mixed up with. Camilla was in need of terminating the baby without the father finding out, and with how desperately she needed our advice, I'm assuming he was a dangerous man," Rodney said, his eyes never leaving Coral's.

A gust of wind passed behind Coral as the bus she needed to get on to go home drove past them and along the road, but Coral didn't run for it. Coral didn't move at all.

12

Wandering along the beaten dirt track on jelly-like legs, her lungs burning as if they'd been set ablaze from running and not stopping, Coral found herself at the garden centre near her village without even realising. Childhood memories of being here flashed up in her mind like breaking news on the TV. She locked eyes on the playground outside and the happy youngsters using all the energy they had and more to make their way to the top of the climbing apparatus, remembering and wishing that she were a child once again, even for just one moment. Innocent, content with the world, and blinded from the horridness of getting older and what the future could hold.

As a child, it's all about living in the moment; the importance of running as fast as you can across the grass, dancing to cheesy pop songs while singing out of tune, stuffing your face with ice cream and jelly till you can't possibly eat anymore, but still going on to consume more anyway. No one prepares you for adulthood; no one tells you of the pain and suffering you go through. But how can they? Who would want to get older if it meant knowing what was to come? It would cause more deaths than anything else. If only life had a pause button or a rewind, then maybe, just maybe, life could be bearable. *Thank God I'm not psychic*, thought Coral. There's no way she would've wanted to grow older and experience any of this if she'd known what was coming.

As she walked through the automatic sliding doors, her breath catching in her throat, the strong earthy smell hit her nose. She felt her body try to relax, but then quickly the anxiety regained power, and she felt herself zooming towards the trolley station, turning and proceeding to rattle her way up and down the aisles holding on tight to the cool plastic of the trolley handle.

Thump. Thump. Thump.

Her pulse pounded loud and clear in her ears, adrenaline fuelling her and keeping her going forwards. She felt like this once when she was a child, making her way through aisle after aisle trying to find her mum and dad after she'd wandered off to see a Christmas display and turned around to find her parents had gone. But this time, she was looking for her past, any thread to hold onto. She needed something to make her feel light and airy again with what she *used to know* instead of weighed down, like the so-called witches were when thrown into the water, with what she knew *now*. She was drowning, suffocating, and blinded by her surroundings, all at once, her thoughts and feelings tumbling out of control as if she'd been thrown into a human-sized washing machine, going round and round and not being able to break out.

One thought kept playing and replaying in her head over and over again.

Her mum had been pregnant.

After the conversation with Rodney had taken place, she'd taken off on unsteady legs, running in the direction of home, no thought process on how she'd get home or even if she knew which twists and turns of the roads to take by running; she had no idea where she was to start with, she just allowed her legs to move and take her as far away from the new truth she had learnt as possible.

How could her mum have kept it to herself? All the hurt she'd gone through, all the pain of being forced into pregnancy without consent? And why hadn't she reported it to the police?

Coral's chest began to ache, her breathing becoming heavier by the second. The woman she thought she knew was becoming the woman she hardly knew at all, and her brain couldn't handle this information. If she hadn't become tangled up with the man who assaulted her, would she still be alive now? Would she be here in this garden centre, buying more flowers and more plants to plant and amaze people with? Who would she be?

Without warning, her body and thoughts came to an abrupt stop. She looked around with crazed eyes as if realising for the first time that she was still pushing the trolley around the aisles of the garden centre rather than running along the country roads back to the village. Her focus regained, and she looked up at what had caused her to stop and wake up from her fast-paced thoughts.

"Coral?" the deep, mellifluous voice asked her, and suddenly the tears started to fall down her face, as if they'd been waiting on the edge, waiting for something to give them the go-ahead to fall and dampen her cheeks. He looked happy but concerned, and once he noticed she was crying, he made his way around the trolley and wrapped his arms around her, engulfing her in the most wonderful hug; the pain she had circling her starting to slightly dim, her breathing beginning to slowly ease. Coral mumbled into his polo shirt.

"What was that?" he asked.

Coral pulled back, wiping her eyes, and looked up into his twinkling eyes, the colour of them reminding her of a chocolate milkshake, something that she wished she had in her hand right now to help cool her down and make her feel even just a tiny bit better.

"Nitis? What are you doing here?"

He smiled and pointed to the garden centre logo on his polo shirt. "I work here; I have done for the last seven months."

"I had no idea..." she trailed off and looked into her trolley, feeling embarrassed.

"Do you need any assistance, miss?" he asked, a smile playing on his lips, gently using the back of his left hand to wipe her stray tears away. "I'm a very keen gardener myself and have plenty of advice I could share with you."

Coral nodded and smiled up at him, understanding he was trying to make her feel better. "My mum loved plants, flowers; all things nature. I want to bring life back into my home. I want her memory to not just be a memory; I want to feel like she's with us, always."

"Are you looking for indoor or outdoor plants?" Nitis asked, taking her left hand and wrapping it around his bicep. She shivered as she felt the warmth under her fingers, her heart rate slowing down peacefully. He placed his hands on the trolley and slowly started to move it forwards.

"Both," Coral replied, "I'll take good care of them too. I'll help them grow, and they'll be beautiful for years."

Nitis let out a soft chuckle which sent shivers throughout her again. "It sounds like you're talking about a baby."

"Nature was my mum's baby," she said. This made Coral smile, the last of her tears falling from her eyes. Nitis looked down at her and smiled too.

"Your mum sounds like the sort of person I wish I could've met."

This made Coral smile even more. "I think she'd have liked you a great deal."

Nitis steered the trolley up and down the aisles, both of them sauntering in calming silence until they were through the automatic sliding doors to the outdoor section of the garden centre. Coral held her free hand up to her eyes to help shield them from the blazing sun, but once her eyes had adjusted, she looked around, and the light and airy feeling once again started to return within her, making happy tears start to blur her vision. An orchestra worth of flowers presented themselves, standing tall and mesmerizing, glowing brighter in colour in the afternoon sunshine making her heart feel full. No wonder her mum loved nature when it looked like this.

"Is it possible to take them all?" Coral asked breathlessly. Nitis once again chuckled. "I mean, I'd probably have to save up for months to afford it, but I'm sure my ninja skills could help me take them all in the dead of night instead."

"I could assist with my ninja skills? Or my seven months' worth of savings," Nitis added, his smile not faltering once.

"Like I'd let you waste your savings on me," Coral mumbled.

"It wouldn't be a waste if it means I'm making you happy," he said, smiling down at her. A flicker of confusion must have etched on her face, so he opened his mouth to speak, thought for a moment and said, "I'd do anything to make you happy, Coral."

With promptness, a throat was cleared, and they both looked apart from one another and focused their attention on a paunchy middle-aged man with a moustache that resembled a sweeping brush's bristles and a shiny bald head that looked to be struggling in the heat. The man cleared his throat once again before speaking. "Nitis, I hope you're not clocking off early," the man said, proceeding to cough into a handkerchief.

"Most definitely not; this young lady needed advice on plants and flowers for her home, and so I was showing her the best flowers we have to offer," Nitis said smoothly, no hesitation laced in his voice.

"It's true," Coral said, turning her attention to the man with sweat trickling down his forehead, "he's being extremely helpful."

The grouchy man, who Coral guessed was Nitis's manager, gave a pointed look towards him before marching off, still coughing into his handkerchief.

*＊＊＊

Coral spent the afternoon waiting outside the garden centre on a bench, going from enjoying the calming breeze and nature around her to watching the happy children being peeled away from the playground and enveloped into their cars to go back home until Nitis meandered out of the automatic sliding doors.

"You waited for me?" Nitis asked, one eyebrow crooked and his lips plastering into an instant smile.

"We were rudely interrupted by your sweaty manager, remember? We have more conversing to do," Coral said, her smile growing by the second.

"Is that just the reason?" he asked.

Coral hesitated and let out a sigh. "I've had a really tough day, and your presence alone is helping me feel less like my world is disintegrating before my eyes."

"Well, since we're going to be on foot, how about I walk you home like the gentleman I am? It would be a shame to waste such a beautiful afternoon on a bus. Then, we can either talk about what's making your world fall apart, or we can talk about anything else instead," he said, holding his arm out once again.

"I'd love that," she said, hooking her hand around his warm bicep, her heart fluttering in her chest, making her feel sprightly and electrified. Everything was just so simple and peaceful with Nitis, no drama, no confusion, pure bliss.

* * * *

The walk home was like something from a film; the air was calming, the grasshoppers had started to chirp, and the cars on the roads had thinned out. Coral hadn't felt this at ease in a long time, especially after everything that had happened today, but the feeling of the sun on her back and the smell of the fresh country air and Nitis's aftershave mixed together; it put all her troubles on hold for just a matter of moments.

"So, are you going to tell me what upset you so much earlier, or am I pretending you didn't soak my polo shirt with your tears?" Nitis asked, his eyes never leaving the path ahead of them, no hint of a smile on his face.

Coral sighed and squinted ahead, recognising the walk hadn't taken as long as she'd hoped and that she was almost back home. "Have you ever thought you knew something for what it was, or someone for whom they were, and you basically get it completely wrong, and you just don't know how to begin to understand what's in front of you anymore?"

Nitis had a questioning look on his face and took a few moments to reply to her. "Sort of... can I ask who or what this is about?"

"My mum," Coral blurted out without a second thought. "I feel like I'm learning more about her now that she's gone than I did when she was alive, and it's changing my idea about the woman I thought I knew before. It's sickening and breaking me piece by piece. I just wish I could speak to her about it all and clear my head."

Nitis stopped, and Coral wondered why until she noticed they were outside her house. *Damn*, Coral thought, *just when my troubles were beginning to fade away into the sunset*. Nitis put a hand on either side of her arms and looked straight into her eyes. "Coral... hear me out. Your mum was *your* mum, but she was also someone's daughter, sister, friend, wife and probably much more. She made her bed, and she lay in it. It was *her* who made the decisions she made, the choices, whether they were good or bad ones. You were young, and whatever she did or didn't do, she wouldn't have burdened you with them at the age you were. You were her little girl; it was her duty to protect you from the evils in this world, and if she'd been here now, who's to say anything would be any different?"

Coral was speechless, so she let him continue.

"Everyone makes their choices; everyone has to accept what they do by living and learning through it, including us. Remember the woman who raised you, not the opinions and stories of others around you. They don't matter. *She* mattered; the woman she was to *you*."

Coral stared up at him with tears in her eyes and gave a small smile. No one other than Iris had ever spoken to her in so much depth and compassion before. He had a point, though. Why should what she'd learnt today change her idea about her mum? Why should it make her question so much? Why did she let the flowers at her mum's grave affect her like it had done and let it lead her to all of this? Yes, her mum was apparently pregnant before she died, but Coral wasn't aware of that until now, and what difference did it make learning that now, so many years after it had happened? Other than the fact her mum had been assaulted by someone and therefore became pregnant, there was nothing else that was overly new to her that should really storm her mind. Her mum was her mum, but that wasn't the only role she had played.

"You make a good point, Nitis," she finally said, letting herself catch her breath once more, the thought of breathing a far-off idea in her mind. "You always seem to make a good point."

"I just want you to be happy, Coral, in all aspects of your life. You deserve the world, and no one should make you think any less," he said and leant down towards her, brushing his lips against her cheek and planting the gentlest of kisses there.

The tingling sensation she got from his touch made her want to wrap her arms around him and press her lips on his, but she decided not to ruin the moment, and exhaustion was beginning to take over her. Sparks were soaring between them, and she didn't want him to leave, but she knew she needed sleep. As if he'd read her mind, he turned to her and cleared his throat, trying to take away the attention from the slight blush in his cheeks.

"Anyway," he said, "I better get going. I'll see you soon, though. You know where I am if you need me."

As he started to walk down the street, Coral called after him, "I didn't buy any plants or flowers."

Nitis turned around and grinned at her, her insides weakening at the sight of it. "Well, we better change that, hadn't we," he said, winking at her and leaving her completely speechless yet again. *How can one human know exactly the right things to say and do to help me feel better in such an effortless way?* she wondered.

Coral wandered up to her front door and pressed her hand down on the handle. Usually, the cold of it pierced her, but this time, it was sort of refreshing, and as she tried to push it open, she realised it was locked. *Strange,* she thought, usually her dad would be in at least, which meant it would be unlocked. Making her way through the contents in her bag, she found her keys and let herself in, letting the coldness of the hallway engulf her as it always did.

I'm feeling inspired, Coral thought, wondering what paints she was going to get out and use on her canvas this time, realising she needed to buy some more to add to her collection. *It's been a while since I painted, and it'll relax me enough to help me sleep at least.* Bounding up the stairs and into her bedroom, ready to take her paintbrushes out, she came to a sudden halt and let out a small shriek, clutching her right fist to her chest to slow down her heart rate. "Dylan! What the fuck?"

"I texted you earlier about coming over but you never replied, so I thought I'd just come over anyway," he said, not moving once from where he was laid on her bed. "That's not usually a problem?"

Coral rolled her eyes and puffed out her cheeks in exasperation. "I've had a rollercoaster of a day, Dylan. What do you want?"

"Wow, and my days been *full* of roses, hasn't it," he half barked at her. Coral raised her eyebrows.

"It isn't a competition to see who has had it worse than the other, you know? I'm allowed to say I've had a shit day without you coming in here and making things worse with your attitude. You know where the window is; just get out."

"Right," he murmured and sat up on the bed, patting the plastic bag next to him. "Anyway, I brought you these. I was having a clear-out of all the things that got left behind by the previous owner of the flat and found some pretty stuff that I thought you might like."

Coral looked down at her feet and then back up at him. "Thanks," she muttered and gave a flicker of a forced smile.

"You're welcome. See? You were about to cause an argument, for no reason, when I was doing something *nice* for you," he said and flashed a sarcastic smile back at her. "Anyway, if you've had it rough, I'll go and leave you to it," he said and started to rise up off of the bed.

"You can take these home with you," she said and walked over to the bin in the corner of her room, plucking the fluorescent green knickers out and throwing them at Dylan. He held them in his hands, turning them over and smirked.

"Take them home with me? So you can wear them next time you come over?" he asked, smirking even more now and making his way over to her, hands at the ready to grab her hips and pull her towards him.

"You mean so the other girl you're banging can wear them next time I'm not around?"

Dylan stopped in his tracks, and the smirk faltered slightly. "What?"

"If you knew me well enough, you'd know what underwear I wear and that you've never *once* seen me in anything fluorescent," she said, marching over to her wardrobe and throwing open the doors, pointing at the clothes in the wardrobe. Coral then did the same to her chest of drawers, pulling open the top drawer to reveal all the black underwear she owned, the only colour to exist in there. "Does any of this scream *I'm a walking talking highlighter* to you?"

"Is this some kind of a joke?" he asked, smirking once again.

"Do I *sound* like I'm in a jokey mood, Dylan? The other night when I woke up at yours, I was trying to find my clothes in the dark so I could leave, and so I pocketed what I *thought* were my knickers and got home to find these which *aren't mine*."

Dylan began sniggering, which made Coral's blood boil even more. "What eighteen-year-old girl still calls them *knickers*?"

"Dylan," she roared at him, "if you're fucking other people, just say!"

"I bought them for you and just threw them onto my bedroom floor. Why does it matter?" he asked, looking angry now. Coral wasn't going to give in easily.

"Bull. Shit. Why isn't there a tag on them then if they're new?"

Dylan stared her out, then walked over to the open window and hooked one leg through before turning towards her. "You're changing, and I don't like it." With that, he was gone.

"I'm changing, and I *love* it," Coral shouted out of the window before slumping down onto her bed and pouring out the contents of the plastic bag next to her. A selection of trinkets landed softly onto her duvet, such as a small Victorian-style candlestick holder, a couple of thimbles, a handful of different sized and coloured buttons, a broken pot doll and a mass of silver and gold jewellery tangled up within each other. *Something to take my mind off of the day*, she thought.

Turning on her CD player and listening to the quiet tinkling of calming synth-pop music, she felt her body relax and laid back on one of her propped-up pillows, ready to put her focus into untangling the mess of jewellery before her.

As Coral made her way through the unknotting of the delicate jewellery, she thought about what Dylan had said. She *was* changing. Before, finding someone else's underwear in Dylan's flat wouldn't have affected her, mostly because she would've taken this opportunity to get revenge and find someone else to flirt with, make out with or just simply get into bed with to get back at him. The Coral laid on this bed right now was angry at the thought of him having the audacity to even *think* about getting into bed with someone else, let alone actually removing their underwear and keeping it in his bedroom as some kind of trophy, and god knows what else he'd done with this other person.

Why was she so badly affected by someone who she wasn't going to stay with forever? All they were to each other were comfort blankets, ready to engulf the other when life was getting too rough for them, smothering them with alcohol, drugs and anything else to take the pain away. But what if, after all this time, Dylan wasn't a comfort blanket? What if he was making things a lot worse, and she'd been blinded because of her messed-up state of mind? What if he'd been adding to the suffocation all along?

As these thoughts swam through her brain, she hooked her finger through one more loop and pulled free one of the pieces of jewellery. "Booyah," she said to herself, punching the air. Sitting up straighter, she dropped down the bundle of jewellery and held up the piece she had pulled free.

Without warning, everything felt like it was suddenly in slow motion, the music from her CD player slowing down, every lyric drawn out, her breathing becoming heavier and deeper by the second, the oxygen struggling to make its way into her lungs.

Coral staggered off of her bed, causing her to tip with the world, grabbing her bin with just enough time to throw up into it, tears stinging her eyes as if they were made from bleach. As she choked out the remainder of the bile in her throat, she slowly crawled back over to her bed and peered onto the duvet at the piece of jewellery she had just untangled. It wasn't just any piece of random discarded jewellery. It was a lost and found piece.

It was her mum's charm bracelet.

13

Coral woke up with a start to the sound of her alarm going off, feeling extremely rough. Carefully rising up from her bed, groaning at the pain in her head, she looked down at her pillow. Gone was the crisp white colour, and coating it was the black tear stains she'd let soak in all throughout the night. The entirety of the night and into the early hours of the morning, crying about the jewellery she had found was all she could do as well as throwing up, crying some more and texting Iris frantically, getting no reply at all. She'd also left Dylan a handful of texts and voicemails about where he had got the bracelet from and who owned the apartment before him, but it was no luck: nobody wanted to reply to her in her time of need.

Lazily, she picked her phone up from the floor and began to scroll through the notifications, only to realise there was only one from Iris, which had been sent to her as a private message on a social media account Coral hardly used. "Weird," Coral said aloud; they only ever texted each other. The message read:

Broke my phone and bogged down with work so I'll get back to you in the next few days.

Even weirder, Coral thought. Iris had never broken a phone before, and she was *never* too busy for Coral; she also most *definitely* never ended her messages with just a full stop; it just wasn't her way of texting at all.

Coral shrugged it off and grabbed her black skirt and white blouse from the chair by the dressing table and tugged them on, taking her time as she had a few hours before sixth form started. She caught sight of the bracelet again but disregarded it, along with the haunting feeling it gave her. *I'll get to the bottom of that later,* she thought, grabbing the empty Jack Daniels bottle from the bedside cabinet. Hesitating, she crouched down onto the floor and grabbed all of the bottles of booze from under her bed, the half-empty cigarette packet from her sock drawer and the two spliffs from her makeup bag, laying them all out on her bed. She then opened up her wardrobe, grabbed an old plastic bag from the depths of it, and turned back to look at the self-destruction equipment on her bed that had ripped apart and robbed her of so many years of her life. If Dylan thought she had changed before, wait until he got a load of *this.*

Picking up the weighed-down plastic bag she had carefully filled with the contents from her bed, Coral made her way down the stairs and placed it on the kitchen worktop.

"You're up early for a Monday morning," Kruze commented, making Coral jump; one of his hands gripped the kettle handle as it bubbled away.

"Enough there for another mug?" Coral asked, signalling with her head towards the kettle. A thoughtful look crossed Kruze's face before he opened the cupboard above him and took out Coral's seashell mug that she always used.

"I see you've been productive this morning," Kruze said, not looking up once while making the mugs of coffee.

"I'm changing," she said, letting the sentence float through the air like a cigarette cloud.

"Coral, I know we said we could talk about anything, but female bodies changing aren't—"

"Kruze! I don't mean it like that..." she said, trailing off.

"Oh," he said, passing her the mug of coffee, steam making its way into the air above it. "I heard you last night, well, the early hours of this morning... you sounded really upset... I wanted to come in, but I know sometimes you like to be alone..." he said, pretending to take a sip of his coffee to take away the awkwardness of the conversation.

"It's okay. Listen, I was watching a film last night, and I wanted to ask, from a policeman's perspective, what you think of the situation that unravelled in one of the scenes."

"Sure, go ahead," Kruze said, leaning back against the worktop.

Coral moved so she was at an angle to him.

"Okay. So a woman died, and the police said it was suicide, but then, years later, the daughter of the woman figures out it could quite possibly *not* have been suicide, and so—"

"Coral, is this about mum?" Kruze asked, sighing and putting down his mug. She didn't say anything; she just nodded and looked up at him from under her eyelashes that were stuck together. "You don't think it was suicide?" he asked.

"I know it sounds crazy and stupid, but I just *know* she didn't kill herself, Kruze. Like everyone said—"

"She loved life, I know," he said. "I remember that being the quote of the year from everyone who'd come to the house after it had happened, or passed us by in the village or spoke to us at the funeral," he said, looking away and taking a deep breath. "So," he started, locking eyes with her, "after all this time, you've opened up."

"What do you mean?" Coral asked in the gentlest voice she had, clearly still half asleep. With only getting a few hours of sleep last night, the exhaustion was still overpowering her, and the puffiness of her eyes didn't help, which caused her to force her eyes to keep blinking in order to stay awake.

"I never believed our own mum would leave us and dad behind. I tried to talk to Aunt Eva about it, but she sounded glad to see the back of her and just kept saying how selfish mum was." He rolled his eyes and locked his jaw so tight she thought it might snap and fall off. "She wasn't selfish... she was beyond *selfless*." Coral took a step back as her brain processed what her brother had just said. All this time, and he'd never believed what the police had told them either, just like she hadn't. He turned around, picked up his mug and said, "Let's go sit in the living room, and you can tell me what you're *really* thinking for once."

Once they'd entered the living room and she'd closed the door behind her, they got sat down on the sofa, and that's exactly what Coral did; she opened up more than she ever had in her life, and she let her body shake as the tears fell down her face and onto her blouse, spilling over and never once letting up. She told him everything, from the moment of finding the flowers with the card attached that set all of this off, to questioning people from the clientele book, to discovering the charm bracelet last night that caused her to be so shook up.

It was a lot to take in, especially saying it all out loud and making the situation so real and alive, and as she looked up at him, she noticed his eyes were burning, red-rimmed, and his cheeks were shiny from the tears he'd let go of.

"I know it's a lot to take in, Kruze..." she said, taking a sip of her coffee.

He let out a breathless noise and wiped his face with his hands.

"Yeah... that's one hell of a bomb you've just dropped," he said, not once looking at Coral. "I'm... I'm not sure what to say... I'm angry... I'm upset... I need a moment," he said, standing up and making his way out of the room.

* * * *

Coral sat quietly for a while, running her fingers through her hair and trying her best to break the knots away. Just as she thought Kruze wasn't going to come back in, he slowly entered and hovered at the door, closing it behind him, probably just so their dad didn't hear what they were talking about.

"What were you going to do next?" he mumbled.

"I wasn't sure, to be honest... I need to ask Dylan about the charm bracelet, but he's not returning any of my calls or texts—"

"Why did that stupid excuse for a human being have *our* mum's charm bracelet anyway?" he asked, his voice rising slightly in volume.

"I've no idea; he just said he was having a clear-out from what the previous owner left behind," she said, taking a big gulp of her coffee now. It was lukewarm, just how she liked it best.

"So that's the question, isn't it really... Who the hell was the previous owner?" Kruze said.

Coral looked at him with the most serious expression she had; she felt more determined than ever before after the newest piece of evidence had been revealed last night. "That's what I'd like to know."

"Well, you picked a good day to open up. Luckily, I don't have work today, so I've got the day to process what you've just told me and try to figure some things out. Whereas you better go get a wash and change your clothes," Kruze said, gesturing towards the tear-stained blouse Coral was wearing. "If Iris isn't available, you've got a trek and a half to walk this morning, but don't worry... we'll figure this out, Coral. We *will* get justice for Mum."

14

Coral reached for the bronze lion door knocker on the bold red door and tapped it three times, taking a step back and wringing her hands together nervously. All day during sixth form, she had been so distracted with wondering about Iris, leaving her voicemail after voicemail, as well as thinking about the conversation between Kruze and herself from the morning, that she hadn't paid any attention to anything going on in her lessons and her mind had been blank to everything else. Molly had tried her best to make conversation with her, but Coral's mind was elsewhere completely, so oblivious to the world around her that she didn't even hear Molly ask her at lunchtime about going over to her house after sixth form had ended; she just nodded to everything she said, so when she received a text from Molly as to what time she could come over, she was confused and suddenly felt very anxious.

It had been a long time since she'd been invited over to someone's home, someone that wasn't Dylan or Iris at least, so she wasn't sure how to act in front of other people or how to even communicate for that long without awkward silences taking over; she was *way* out of her comfort zone. Coral knew deep down she had to try; she needed to develop her communication skills and confidence in uncomfortable situations, but she didn't feel like it was the right time to, even with someone as kind and lovely as Molly.

Maybe I should go home, she thought, but as she was about to turn around and leave, the door swung open to reveal Molly's beaming face staring at her surprised one; every feature on her face as excited as a child's was at Christmas time, unlike Coral's who looked as white as a sheet as if she'd seen a ghost, her mouth hanging slightly open.

"Oh my goodness, you actually showed up. I'm *so* excited that you're here," she said, grabbing Coral's hand and pulling her into the hallway. *No escaping now,* Coral thought. "So, the rule is: shoes off at the door, please, wash your hands in the sink in the kitchen and then get stuck into the delicious food."

Coral did as Molly said and left her trainers at the front door neatly on the shoe rack. She then followed her into the kitchen, anxiously washing her hands with the bubble gum scented soap in the sink, and proceeded to take her seat at the table.

"So, *you* must be Coral," a tall woman with age spots and over-dyed brown hair said as she walked into the kitchen, opening up the oven and sliding out a Pyrex dish. "I've heard so much about you."

Coral started to pick at the skin on her thumb. "Hopefully, all good things," she shakily replied. *Pull yourself together, girl,* she thought to herself. *This situation isn't as bad as you think it is.*

"Oh definitely; Mol says you're like the sister she always wanted," Molly's mum said, using a knife to cut the food up equally, then using a flat utensil to serve it onto three plates. Coral felt her body relax slightly, a warm feeling rising within her; Molly really did value their friendship.

"Mum, *stop*, that's embarrassing," Molly said, covering her face while giggling. She then leant forward and whispered to Coral, "I hope you like lasagne."

Coral grinned, and her eyes glowed as she replied, "It's actually my favourite."

"Well, I'm more than happy to hear that," Molly's mum said, putting down a plate of lasagne in front of Coral and a bowl of salad in the centre of the table. "Help yourself to salad. I know it's not everyone's go-to choice, but it's a good combination I find."

Coral wasn't a fan of salad and always took it out of her meals, scraping it to the side of her plate every time, but tonight, she felt it was a different scenario, so she used the tongs and dropped pieces of lettuce, tomato and cucumber onto her plate; she had to be a polite guest. Once Coral had placed the tongs back down, Molly's mum took a seat at the end of the table and started helping herself from the salad bowl.

"So, Mol tells me you're working on a project together?"

"Yeah," Coral said, chewing the piece of lasagne she put in her mouth as quickly as she could and swallowed, despite the heat, so she could reply properly. "But I think Molly will have done better than I have so far. I get distracted with the world around me way too easily."

"Don't worry, I've found too many pieces of writing to even start it as I can't pick which one to use; I'm spoilt for choice. I'll show you what I've found so far after we've eaten," Molly said, halfway through her food already.

Coral wasn't used to eating so much, usually filling her belly with alcohol and scraps of nibbles from the cupboard instead, but it felt good to have a hearty meal in front of her for a change, so she tried her best to make her way through the meal without seeming ungrateful; ignoring the ache in her stomach from overeating compared to what her body was used to.

"Honestly, love," Molly's mum said, putting her hand softly next to Coral's as if she'd read her mind, "if you're too full, don't force it down your throat. The portions were really big anyway, we're just greedy me and Mol," she said, winking at her.

Coral smiled but continued to eat, feeling emotional at how kind Molly and her mum were, how good the food tasted and how she'd missed eating properly for the last five years. This lovely woman, who she'd only just met, had made her so much delicious food from the kindness of her heart, and she couldn't be more grateful.

* * * *

After almost clearing her plate and making general chit chat with Molly's mum, Coral and Molly excused themselves to go upstairs into Molly's bedroom. As Coral made her way through the house, she noticed that the environment around her was pristine and full of plants, bright yellow walls and not a piece of furniture out of place. Taking a deep breath in, she let the lavender scent fill her lungs, and her body relaxed and eased as she made her way up the stairs and through the pearlescent white bedroom door.

"Feel free to have a lie-down," Molly motioned towards the bed, "I'm currently in a food coma and about to collapse," she said, proceeding to flop onto her bed dramatically. Coral, feeling much more relaxed after the conversations at the table, joined in and gently made her way onto Molly's bed beside her and started laughing.

"Honestly, Molly, I can't remember the last time I ate so much that I felt this full," Coral said, rubbing her stomach. "That lasagne was something else; your mum's so good at cooking, but now I feel like I'm about to give birth to everything I've just eaten."

Molly started giggling and looked at her. Something triggered in them, and suddenly they both burst into a random fit of hysterics as if they were full on laughing gas, holding their stomachs and groaning.

Coral sat up on her elbows, taking in the room and how bright it was. Each wall was painted white, but they were covered in rainbow flags of every size, and clusters of photos hung from string and pegs strewn across the walls. "So you're a fan of rainbows..." she started but stopped in her tracks as her eyes found a photograph on the bedside table of Molly and a blonde girl; Molly's arms wrapped around the blonde, kissing one of her freckled dimpled cheeks. "Oh..." she said, slowly casting her eyes on Molly. "I didn't know."

Molly started laughing and sat up at the same time that Coral did, grabbing the picture and smiling down at it. "Don't worry, I didn't invite you over so I could seduce you and get you into my bed" she said, laughing and holding the photograph close to her chest. "But yes, she's the best thing that's happened to me in a very long time. We were friends for years, and one day I just leant in and kissed her, hoping she felt the same. The smile on her face when she kissed me back was confirmation enough for me."

"When did you know you were..." Coral didn't finish off the sentence, unsure which word to use.

"Gay? Lesbian? Batting for the ladies' team? It's okay to say it, Coral," Molly said, placing a gentle hand on her arm, "I haven't always been that way inclined."

"Oh, right; when did you realise?"

"Well, I was at a party years ago, and the guy I was into tried to take advantage of me. He led me into a room, and we were kissing and it was really nice. I was so happy, I'd waited so long to kiss him and it was finally happening." Without warning, Molly's face drained of colour and she looked down, playing with the hem of her sleeve. "But then both he and his friend tried to pin me down so that he could, well... you can imagine what he wanted to do to me. They were laughing and saying disgusting things to me about what was about to happen, saying I was asking for it for wearing such a tight dress... I screamed and screamed, and luckily someone walked in just as the guy I liked had pulled my underwear down and put... put it in me..." Molly trailed off, looking down, her hands shaking.

Coral's jaw dropped, unable to comprehend what she had just been told. *Who the hell would do such a horrible thing?* Coral wondered. Anger started pulsating through her veins. "Who did this to you?" Coral asked through gritted teeth.

Molly held up her hands. "Honestly, I'm over it, Coral. I've got Faye now, and I'm happy with her, and life isn't as bad as it was back then. I'm just glad he didn't get chance to go any further. I can't even imagine..." Molly trailed off, shaking her head. "It was enough to put me off men instantly," she continued. "I know not every guy is that way inclined, but that experience was enough for me."

Slowly standing up, she put the photograph back down on her bedside table and then switched on the fairy lights that were wrapped around her metal bed frame. "Anyway, never mind that... how've you been? I know it was the anniversary for your mum recently."

Coral stared into space. How had she not known what Molly had gone through until now? No wonder she was so quiet and timid in sixth form; she probably didn't trust a soul. "Sorry," she said, looking at Molly, then back down at the floor, shaking her head from the thoughts that were distracting her and flying around in her mind. "Yeah, I'm okay. I wasn't, but... I'm trying to see more positives in life which, in turn, is hard. I feel like I'm changing, though."

Turning to Molly, she looked into her eyes and took a deep breath, ready to continue explaining her feelings, but on a deeper level this time, like she never had before. "I'll be honest with you, even though you've probably figured all this out by now; I'm going to be completely honest about myself no matter how hard it is to say it all."

"You don't have to say anything you feel uncomfortable saying, Coral; it's okay," Molly said in a soothing tone.

Coral considered this but shook her head. "No. I need to open up and get this load off of my chest and face the reality of it all," she said, taking a deep breath once again and focusing her mind on how to make the words in her head come out of her mouth in a non-complicated way. "I drink alcohol every day and have done for years. I smoke so I can fill my lungs with something other than the suffocation of grief. I dye my hair so I don't look like the ghost of my own mum, and

I have a boyfriend that practically just uses me to make himself feel better, never checking up on me when I need him most and probably sleeping with half of the most desperate girls in the village. My brother works hard to make sure we have a roof over our heads which pushes him to breaking point, and I'm surprised my dad's still alive with the length of time he's locked himself away in his bedroom."

Coral could see the girl before her was trying to take in everything she was hearing, and she had to admit, she wasn't sure what she expected to hear in response from her friend; Molly's attentive eyes never left hers. Coral continued. "Grief is a killer, and I've been a walking zombie for years and somehow, I'm still alive, but I haven't felt *alive*, Molly; not for a long time. But... I'm ready for change to take over. I'm ready to change who I am and come back to life and be *me* again."

Taking a steady breath, Coral wiped the tears that had streamed down her face while speaking and cleared her throat as Molly took her hands in hers, giving her a compassionate smile. "God knows how I'm still alive," Coral whispered. "No wonder no one at school ever became friends with me. Who wants to be friends with the broken girl?" Coral looked up at her friend's face; her warm, kind eyes, her gentle smile, no hint of the shock and disgust she assumed would be there like it was on everyone else's face that surrounded her.

"When I was seven years old," Molly said, no hesitation in her voice, "there was an afternoon where I spent it baking with my mum in the kitchen. My dad had taken my little twin brothers to their first party; the party was for a friend of theirs from the nursery they went to. I couldn't wait for them to come home so

I could hear their excitement about the party games and all the cake they'd eaten." Molly smiled down at her lap, fondly remembering the memory. "Unfortunately, I never got to hear their high-pitched excitable voices again or hear my dad's calming voice either. They were walking back home from the party when a driver, who was too busy texting on his phone, headed straight towards my little family. They were pronounced dead the moment the police and paramedics turned up. So believe me, I understand long-term grief."

Coral didn't mean to, but she sat, once again, with her mouth gaping open, tears burning her eyes, making her blink repeatedly. She was shell shocked. This girl, who in the beginning Coral had found beyond annoying, was just as broken as she was, and she'd had *no* idea.

Molly continued. "I've been seeing a therapist ever since, and so has my mum. Our lives changed that day, and I've been to hell and back plenty of times. Our little family of five should've *always* remained five, but there was nothing I could've done to prevent it," she said, squeezing Coral's hand tightly, "and there's *nothing* you could've done either, Coral. You were a good daughter in the days your mum was alive; you *must* remember that. We're allowed to go off the rails sometimes, we're allowed to feel angry and upset and abuse our bodies sometimes, but we have to learn to be better than the grief. We have to be *stronger* than the grief that tries to consume us. We can't let it consume us for the rest of our lives, otherwise we won't have a life, and we're only young, Coral. Make those we've lost proud of who we've become since their passing and live on for them in the fullest way we can."

By this point, Molly's eyes were full of tears, while Coral's eyes had completely let the tears roll down and soak her cheeks, leaving her skin looking as shiny as it would if she were wearing sun cream. She'd become friends with Molly in such a short space of time and yet learnt so much about her and the pain and suffering she'd gone through. This girl actually *liked* Coral; no pretence, no pressure, just pure friendship growing by the day. Coral wasn't alone in the grief she faced every day; she had plenty of support around her, she just didn't fully know and appreciate what it looked like until now. The blindfold of gloom and pain that had covered her eyes for years was slowly beginning to slip away.

Coral did something she couldn't stop herself from doing and leapt forward, wrapping her arms around her friend's body and whispering to her, "Thank you. I needed that." Molly held her just as tightly, stroking Coral's hair, neither of them letting go of the other, comforting each other with pure kindness.

* * * *

After they'd had their heart-to-heart moment and regained composure, Molly headed downstairs and grabbed a tub of ice cream from the freezer and two spoons. Once she had brought it back upstairs for her and Coral to share, Coral used the remote and looked through the selection of films on the television for them to watch. She settled on a chick flick that Molly had already seen plenty of times, just so it pleased Molly, and so they could still talk throughout the film without being bothered about what was happening on the screen.

As the first scoop of ice cream hit the back of Coral's throat, Molly started flicking through photos on her phone of her and Faye to show her; they were either smiling or pulling silly faces together. She was happy, and Coral was content knowing Molly had found her happiness after what had happened to her. It was rare Coral ever felt happy for anyone that she wasn't close to, but she'd grown very fond of Molly in such a short space of time, and so this was a nice change for her. *The new me,* Coral thought.

"So, who's your lover boy?" Molly asked, nudging Coral's arm playfully.

"More like a half-hearted excuse for a male," Coral said, rolling her eyes. "So bold of you to assume I just have the one lover boy anyway, or maybe I have a lover girl also." Coral winked at Molly.

"Trust me," Molly started, shifting positions so she was closer to Coral, "I've got a lesbian radar programmed into me; I'd know if you were batting for the same team as me, missus," she giggled, trying to scoop out some ice cream with her spoon. "So, have you got any photos together you could show me?"

Coral wiggled her phone out of her pocket and scanned through her pictures to try and find one. Dylan and Coral never really took photos together, so it was a challenge trying to locate one. She settled on one taken at a party, the party where they met. As she held the phone up to Molly, Coral watched as her friend's face went from happy and curious to pure fear in a matter of seconds.

"Molly?" she asked, feeling confused.

"That's... surely that's not... He can't be your boyfriend, right? You're joking," Molly stuttered, her hands shaking.

Confusion etched Coral's face. *Why is she reacting like this?* Coral wondered. "Yeah, people have told me before that he's definitely punching above his weight—"

"No, no, no," Molly said, shaking her head, beginning to scratch her arms with her nails, drawing white lines up and down them, "that's not what I meant... that boy... that *evil* boy..." Molly stuttered again, drifting off and hugging her knees up to her chest; she looked absolutely terrified.

"What do you mean by *evil*?" Coral asked, a slight feeling of frustration sparking in her, unable to understand her friend's reaction. She knew Dylan was an idiot but *evil*?

"I don't want you to flip out at me," Molly whispered.

"Molly, believe me, I'm not going to flip out. Everyone has their own opinions on people."

"Okay... promise me, though?"

"I promise I won't flip out. Now tell me why you're so worked up," Coral said, placing a gentle hand on Molly's shoulder.

"Okay... he's the boy who held me down for his friend to... you know... at the party... That's what he was wearing that night... when he..." Molly drifted off.

Coral stared at Molly as if she'd just been told that the sky had been red all this time and that the grass was actually made of sugar paper, her mouth hanging open once again completely aghast. What had started off as one of the nicest evenings for her in a long time had quickly demolished and become one of the *worst*, or at least one of the worst ways to end it.

Dylan had helped his friend sexually assault Molly, and yet Coral had happily given herself up to Dylan without a second thought that same night without knowing what had happened moments before to this beautiful soul now quivering in front of her. What if Coral had said no? Would he have tried to pin her down and cop a feel, or worse, too?

"I've got to go," Coral said, moving quickly off of the bed, anger propelling her down the stairs to get her trainers back on.

"No, Coral, please don't go," Molly said, hastily following behind her, making her way down the stairs as quickly as she could, slipping on the last step. "He'll retaliate if you say anything to him about it. He'll come after me."

Coral stood up to her full height and looked Molly straight in the eye, not breaking eye contact once. "He wouldn't *dare*. I promise, Molly, I won't let him hurt you again, or anyone else for that matter, and from this moment on, he's *nothing* to me."

* * * *

As she stepped through her front door, the house sounded eerily quiet to Coral, but when didn't it? As she raced up the stairs and her foot hit the top step, she spun around in pure astonishment and gripped the handrail, alarmed at the sound of pottery smashing. As she let her eyes focus on the front door that had just swung open and smashed into an old potted house plant behind it, anxiety suddenly flooded her body, making her feel hot and clammy.

"What the *fuck* are you doing here? Did you follow me home?" Coral shouted to Dylan as he strode manically up the stairs and pushed his way past her, heading straight into her bedroom. Hot on his trail, she followed him, stunned by his destructive entrance, and grabbed the back of his t-shirt completely fuelled with rage. He was usually so sneaky; clearly he didn't care anymore. "Dylan, you're clearly deaf as well as dumb; I *asked*, what are you *doing* here?"

Dylan spun around and looked straight into Coral's eyes. Apart from the first time they had met, her drunken mind clouding her judgement completely at that time, she had never seen him look so *alive*. The grey, rough skin he usually had was now the original tanned he used to be, and the spark in his eyes had returned, and they were glistening, but in a feral way. This was the Dylan she had first met, apart from one thing; he was enraged, just as much as she was.

"I've come for my guitar," he said in an agitated tone with more than a hint of frustration. *What has he done with the drugged-up Dylan who I usually come into contact with?* Coral wondered.

"Well, you could've just *asked* me and I'd have given you it; you didn't need to barge in and start breaking things," Coral said. "You can buy another house plant for our hallway too. Perfect timing, though; you're the unlucky sod I was going to pay a visit to, returning all of the crap that you left in my bedroom." Coral could see his shoulders rising and falling at such a quick pace it could've easily seemed like he was going to erupt. "What's *wrong* with you?"

"What's wrong with *me*? I'm fed up of your *shit* and this *stupid* thing we have going on between us." Coral felt her eyes widen in surprise, her eyebrows springing up.

"A relati—"

"A relationship? Is that what you were going to call this? There's no way you can call it that, Coral, honestly, wake up. We've never been in a relationship because we've never done things like normal people do when they're together. We've never been on a date, we've never talked about our future together, we've never held hands, and we've never truly loved each other. We came together because we had one common interest: both of our home lives were fucked up, and so were we. I came away from my dysfunctional home and climbed through the window of yours so I had someone to understand me."

Coral stared at him in utter disbelief.

"Familiar surroundings; that's what you were to me," he continued. "We had sex, got drunk and got high together. That's all we were for each other. Nothing more, every day, the same routine, and we got by. But if you're going around screwing other people—"

"Wait, *what*?! Who else is there, Dylan? You're the one screwing other people, not me," Coral shouted, stamping her foot down in protest. She would *not* be made out to be the bad guy in all of this.

"You know who. I know all about him, no matter what *lies* you try to feed me. Not like I'm bothered anyway because yes, you're right, Coral, I *have* been with someone else; Becca."

This stung Coral without warning, her eyes widening in shock even more, so much she thought they'd stick like that permanently. "Who is Becca? Is she an imaginary girlfriend of yours or the name of your blow-up doll?" Coral's voice couldn't sound calm no matter how much she tried to contain herself; anger was flowing through her more powerfully than the blood was. "Or is she another girl for you and your friend to pin down and try to *rape*?" The words left Coral's mouth before she had a chance to realise what she'd said. Out of the corner of her eye, she could see that Dylan's loosely hung hands were slowly balling into fists. Coral started to back out of her bedroom and onto the landing. No way was she going to let him hit her.

"What did you just say to me?" he spat at her.

"I know what you did to a girl at that party the night we met," she said. This was her chance to fight against Dylan and the horrible person he was, and to do what was right for Molly. As he opened his mouth to speak, she continued without letting him get a word in first. This was *her* time to communicate the hard, painful truth. "I *know* you and your friend pinned down a girl, and you helped your friend hurt her when she didn't want it. I bet that hurt your ego when she turned you both down, didn't it, Dylan? I bet you felt *small* and *weak*, just like you truly are." Nothing could stop Coral now; she was in the zone she'd spent years only wishing she could be in, strength radiating from her like a roaring fire. "Well, good luck to this Becca. If she knew what was good for her, she'd leave scum like you behind, just like I should've done years ago."

Despite Dylan's tall, rugged stance, she felt brave and tough like a giant would do when they were moments away from squishing an ant-sized human. However, instead of an angry snarl plastered to his face, a twisted smile crept on in its place; he looked menacing. "Oh, she wanted it; she just couldn't handle two of us at the same time, let alone one of us; she had him pull out before she even got to the good part. I'm sure Becca would enjoy it. Plus, she's actually a really nice girl who doesn't just use me for my *talents*."

"What talents are these? You never showed *me* them. Unless you mean lasting a lousy two minutes in bed, but I wouldn't write that on your CV if I were you."

"Fuck off, Coral," he spat at her once again, stepping closer to her. "Becca has a big heart, and she *loves* me; she worships the ground I walk on. I don't get what that other boy even sees in you," Dylan said as he stepped even closer to Coral, causing her to knock her back into the bannister, his knuckles so tightly clenched they were showing pure white as if the skin could start splitting at any given moment. "You're just a stupid—"

Dylan's sentence was interrupted as Coral's dad stepped out through his bedroom door, and in one swift movement, his fist connected with Dylan's face at full force. He fell to the floor, just near the top step, and then looked up, holding his cheek, truly horrified.

"What the hell?" he screeched at him.

Jayden looked scary but very much more alive than he had in the past five years. It made Coral feel faint. She hadn't even noticed his door open and most certainly wasn't aware he was in there, but then again, it wasn't as if there were a long list of places he could hole himself up in within the house. "If I hear you talk to my daughter like that *ever* again, or even come within a *mile* of her or this family, I'll make sure you can't use any of your imaginary talents ever again, boy. Now get the *hell* out of my house."

"Fuck this," Dylan murmured as he scrambled down the stairs, cradling his jaw, and charged out of the front door, swinging it closed behind him.

Coral and Jayden stood in silence for a few moments. "Let's go sit in the living room," Jayden said, moving cautiously down the stairs.

Coral slowly followed behind him, still stunned by what had just happened. It had been so long since they'd shared the living room together. They sat down at either end of the sofa and shared a few silent minutes before the ice was broken between them. "I know I haven't been the best dad to you since your mum passed away, but I couldn't just sit there and listen to that scumbag talk shit about my daughter. I hope he gets castrated so he can't create any more vermin like himself."

"It's okay, Dad—"

"No, Coral, it's not okay," Jayden said, a very firm voice projecting out of his mouth compared to his usual spaced-out voice or just the silence on the other side of his bedroom door. "I just want you to understand that I never wanted it to be like this. I never wanted to be holed up in the house like this, away from you and Kruze, practically abandoning you both. I just couldn't come to terms with how your mum... how she could've just... I thought I was enough... I thought all three of us were enough..." Jayden rubbed at his tired eyes and lowered his head.

Coral's eyes stung from the unexpected tears pricking at her eyes, daring to spill over. She'd let loose so many tears recently; she was unsure how there were any more left to come out.

All these years, her dad had been cooped up in his room with all these wounding thoughts stabbing at his mind in such a tortuously slow way, and yet he'd not told a soul about it. Hiding away in the shadows of the bedroom he used to share with her mum would never have helped, but he had no other choice; constantly having his mind eaten away at and making him blame himself every day for not being enough or doing enough to help when she was still alive.

"Dad, we all have these thoughts; I have them nearly every day, but we can't punish ourselves for what happened; it wasn't our fault," Coral said, and then she thought about what Molly had said to her and decided her dad should hear it also. "We can't let the grief consume us forever. We have to make her proud of who we've become since her passing and live on for her in the fullest way we can. Even though we haven't got her the justice she deserves yet, there's still time to change that, Dad."

Jayden looked at his daughter, eyes red and cheeks wet from silent tears that had made their way down his face. "Coral, I can honestly say to this day that there were no signs of her hating her life so much that she'd choose out of this world. Everything was working out so well here, and our marriage was brilliant... Well, I thought it was—"

"Do you ever wonder if she did kill herself?" the words left Coral's lips involuntarily before she had time to stop herself from speaking them.

"What do you mean?" Jayden asked. Coral opened her mouth to reply when she was interrupted by her mobile buzzing in her pocket. When she looked at the screen, she pressed the answer call button as quick as her fingers would let her.

"Iris, you haven't replied to me for so long. Where've you been? I'm just talking to my dad about things, but I need to talk to—" Coral started, but she suddenly realised it wasn't Iris on the other end of the phone.

It was Iris's mum, sobbing down the phone, pure heartbreak in her voice. After she got Luciana to calm down, she listened to what she had to say and hung up, her body quickly flooding with a deep, cold sensation as if someone had just thrown her into the freezing icy Antarctic waters.

"What's happened?" Jayden asked, regaining composure.

"Can you drive me to the hospital, please? It was Luciana on the phone."

Jayden waited for Coral to speak again; she opened her mouth but struggled for any words to come out. "Coral, what is it?"

"Iris has been viciously attacked," she replied, feeling completely numb. "They've had to admit her to hospital."

15

Coral and her dad didn't speak for the entire journey to the hospital, looking straight ahead through the windscreen the whole time, watching the sudden cloud burst and the traffic blocking their way no matter which route they took. Her heart was beating so hard she thought it would split her chest in half; her brain was too numb to think, she could only feel, and that was enough of a struggle.

Luciana had sounded beyond distressed on the phone, as if she'd just had a limb removed. Speaking way too fast for Coral to comprehend, she tried her best to understand, but it had been difficult to make out what she'd been saying to her. Luckily, she managed to catch the fact that Iris was in hospital from a vicious attack of some sort. But what Coral couldn't understand was how could *anyone* want to attack someone like Iris? Unless it was an animal attack, but the chances of that were *very* slim. However, the chances of a person attacking Iris were extremely unlikely, too. She got on with everyone, and no one stood out as a prime suspect that would've or could've wanted to hurt her for any reason.

Once the hospital was in sight, Jayden pulled into the car park and found a parking space as near to the entrance as he could.

"I'll wait here for you," he said to her, placing his hand over hers and giving it a gentle squeeze before returning it to the wheel.

"Are you sure? I could be a while, that's all."

"Take all the time you need; I'm not going anywhere."

Coral smiled up at him and resisted the urge to hug him. He'd only just opened his bedroom door and left the house after all this time; she didn't want to overwhelm him.

Hearing those words come from her dad's mouth had been strange yet so comforting; it was all she'd wanted for years from him, and so she abandoned the negative thoughts, put her right hand on his left and gently squeezed. It was the jolt of positivity and hope she needed to make her legs move and go into the hospital.

* * * *

Scanning the corridors with a hand against her chest, trying her best to calm her heart down before it exploded, she finally spotted the corridor with Luciana in, talking frantically to a nurse. Her arms were flailing everywhere as she asked as many questions as she possibly could in a matter of seconds, the odd Spanish word getting thrown into the mix in exasperation.

As Coral drew closer, Luciana looked over and ran at her, wrapping her arms around her, squeezing her tighter than she thought was humanly possible and sobbing so powerfully, Coral thought she was going to give way from the force of emotion.

"Coral, thank goodness, you need to try to talk to her, please, you *need* to," Luciana said in a hurried manner. "She won't talk to me, the nurses, or anyone. I need to know what happened to her."

"What do you mean she won't *talk* to you?"

Luciana held Coral at arm's length, tightly gripping her shoulders. "Coral... please... my baby is hurt... please," Luciana said just as she burst into, what was most likely, the hundredth time of yet another flood of tears. She was too young to remember how distraught Luciana had been once she'd lost Matías, only ever knowing her to be happy and full of life; it was truly heartbreaking for Coral to see her this way.

Coral stood up straighter, pushing her shoulders back and took a deep breath to regain focus. Anger was still fuelling her from her chat with Molly earlier and then her standoff with Dylan in her home, but she'd do all she could right now to help her second family.

"Luciana, where did you find her?"

The delicate woman in front of her wiped at her eyes and shook her head.

"Aaron called me; he found her, scooped her up into the car and drove her here. I was at work... I just left and came straight here... Coral... she's a mess."

Coral gripped hold of Luciana's hands and ran her thumbs over the soft skin of her knuckles.

"I'll help in every way that I can," she whispered and gently let go.

With anxiousness rippling throughout her body, she slowly pushed open the door to where her best friend lay in her hospital bed, wrapped up in a hospital gown, wires attached to most sections of her upper body and an oxygen mask over her face. But that wasn't what made Coral let out a silent sob so her friend wouldn't hear her. It was the deep scars on her once flawless cheeks, the bruising around her neck so deep in colour it looked like a fresh tattoo, and a plaster cast wrapped around her left arm. Coral quickly wiped the tears from her face and turned her shaking hands into fists to try to control herself.

She could do this.

She had to.

"Iris? It's me, Coral."

Iris's eyelids slowly fluttered open, scanning the room carefully till they landed on Coral, then they squeezed shut again, tears slowly following, drifting down her cheeks.

"Come on now, girl... I know you hate what you look like right now, and I know you don't want me looking at you, but you're still the most beautiful human on this planet in my eyes," Coral said with a shaky voice, sitting on the padded chair next to Iris's bed, taking her hand in hers. "Listen, your mum told me you won't talk to anyone... I understand that, you've gone through a great deal by the looks of things. With that said, you *need* to try to communicate with me, okay? We need to know who did this to you... I won't settle until I know who it was and see them sent down. Okay?"

Coral tried her best to stop the tears from dripping down her face but was failing horrendously.

Iris slightly moved her head from side to side. She didn't want to speak.

"Iris, I promise you; no one is going to hurt you again. We just want to help."

Iris didn't speak; the tears continued to slide down her face one after the other as if they were racing to leave her eyes.

"Blink twice if you understand what I'm saying."

Iris gently opened her eyes once more, looking over towards her friend with great effort, and blinked twice.

"Good... Now, I understand it's probably hard to speak, so we'll continue with the blinking if you feel more comfortable that way. Do you know who did this to you?"

Iris blinked twice and slowly lifted a finger, ever so slightly, pointing to where her clothes lay in a neat pile in the corner of the room.

"Your clothes?" Coral asked, and once again, Iris blinked twice. Standing up and moving over towards the chair where Iris's clothes were, she picked up the navy-blue pencil skirt and then found the matching navy blazer with the dragonfly brooch on.

"I'm not sure what you want me to do with your clothes," Coral said, but Iris didn't respond.

Coral looked at the clothes in her hand. She held up the pencil skirt, twisting it around, but there was nothing on it, and there were no pockets to explore. Placing it back down, she held up the matching navy blazer and noticed two outside pockets but irritably found they were empty. *Maybe there's an inside pocket*, she thought, and as she slid her hand against the smooth, silky material, she carefully slid her fingers into the inside pocket on the left side. Without warning, her heart began picking up pace again when her fingers clasped around what felt like thick paper, but when she pulled it out and opened it up, it was a photograph.

The room spun, and she quickly moved over to the seat next to Iris and fell down onto it, her hands shaking like she had her fingers clenching onto ice, her brain swimming out of control; the bile once again rising in her throat like it seemed to enjoy doing recently.

"No way..." she whispered breathlessly, one arm holding onto the arm rest, attempting to steady herself, the other still clinging onto the photograph, her eyes unable to stop staring.

All of a sudden, she was aware of how quickly her heart was racing. All the lights that were so dim and broken in her mind suddenly lit up in front of her like a spotlight shining in her eyes, the loose ends all tied up neatly together, the creases of the past ironed out, all of the stars aligning and all of the unknown answers to her questions from the last few years were finally answered in a matter of seconds.

What Coral held in her hands was a photograph of two people together; one person was Coral's mum, and the other was the person who attacked Iris.

But now, looking at the photograph and feeling frozen in time, she realised something else, something that caused her to know that her instant gut feeling at looking at this person in the photograph was correct.

This person didn't just attack Iris.

This person killed Coral's mum.

16

Coral sat back in the armchair in Iris's living room, one she'd never sat in before. Over the years, she'd always sat in one corner of the three-seater sofa, engulfed by it, blending in best she could, but this time, she didn't want to blend in. She wanted to stand out and be the centre of attention in the room, all eyes on her. Deep down, she knew she could do this, especially if she worded everything right and didn't forget any details. There was only one shot for this to work, a very short window of time; there was no space for faults to be made. Coral had rehearsed over and over in her head what she was going to say the minute the disgraceful human walked in.

"Lady Latina, I'm home," the self-assured voice called out as Coral heard him enter the house, stopping her train of thought and causing a sickening feeling in her stomach to begin spreading its way through her. As he walked into view, he stopped abruptly, and his smile faltered ever so slightly, but just enough for Coral to notice.

"Coral?" Aaron asked, a natural smile creeping over his face. Looking her over, his eyebrows lifted as he took in the change in how he usually saw her compared to what she looked like now; she was typically in her army boots; but not today. This day, she was in a pair of heels. "Whoa... you look... very different," he said, swallowing hard, looking around the room in a curious way, still holding onto looking as relaxed as he could in this strange situation.

It was as if he was looking out for hidden cameras or a surprise of some kind, ready for it to jump out at him, which technically was about to happen, but verbally. "The girls aren't here by the looks of things," he said, still looking around the room and then focusing his attention back on her. "How did you get in? Are you staying for dinner?"

Coral shifted in her seat and stood up carefully, smoothing down her black dress, trying her best to calm the adrenaline trying to pump its way throughout her body.

"They went out to get food for tonight," Coral lied. He knew just as well as she did where they both were, but if he was going to play pretend, then so would she. "I was already here, so I said I'd stay while they were out shopping, so I didn't have to traipse back home."

"Why did you choose to dress up for dinner? You haven't done before," he said, looking her up and down.

"I wanted to make an effort. But my actual reasoning for being here is because I was hoping to talk to you," Coral said, feeling a sudden sense of calm and confidence wash over her; she couldn't let any nerves show. She *had* to show who had the upper hand here, and it couldn't be him.

Aaron raised an eyebrow, clearly surprised, but of course he would be; she only ever spoke to him to be polite when she was around to see Iris, making general conversation to fill in any awkward silences when in his presence, but usually Iris or Luciana didn't leave much chance for that to happen. Never had she *wanted* to speak to him for any particular reason, especially on her own, and she wished so hard she didn't need to now. In all of the years she'd known him, he'd always been so relaxed and kind, no hint of anything sinister within him. *It's amazing what a mask can hide*, Coral thought.

"What would you want to talk to me about?" he asked, his eyebrows now pulled tightly together in confusion. Coral cleared her throat, gaining composure by the second. She really hoped her mum could hear and see her at this moment, witnessing the woman she'd become, and somehow send her the strength she needed to do what she had come here to do. She *had* to do this, no matter what the cost was; she'd come too far to turn back now.

"Well, as much as I love throwing paint at a blank canvas, I've realised it's not my calling in life. I want to be a detective, but in order to do that successfully, I have to also be a good historian," Coral said, smiling knowingly. "I want to re-open cases that have happened and replay them with new clues that I find out, shedding a different light on things, maybe even solving unsolved mysteries."

"And you've come to me because...?" Aaron asked with a questioning tone in his voice.

"Well, I know you used to be in the detective line of work yourself some time ago, right?"

"Correct, but that was a long time ago; I'm not entirely sure how much help I could be. I'm a bit rusty," Aaron said, shifting from one stance to another, looking slightly uncomfortable with where this conversation was going.

Coral ignored this and used it to her advantage; she was glad he was uncomfortable, and it was only the start of how uncomfortable she was going to make him feel.

"I've been working on one recently. Could you listen to my ideas for me and give me your opinion at least?"

Aaron looked at her, still surprised, with eyebrows now raised to the ceiling. He gave her a generous smile, sitting down in the armchair opposite her. He looked like he was beginning to feel at ease again, but the cogs had started turning; Coral was sure of that.

"Sure, of course, go ahead," he said, motioning his hand out for her to begin.

"Good," Coral said and began slowly pacing the room in front of him. This was her moment.

"What's the case you were thinking you could re-evaluate?" Aaron asked, sitting back in his chair, hands clasped tightly together, clearly just humouring her. He always seemed to take what Coral said with a pinch of salt, finding her somewhat humorous, which usually she would try to be in order to mask how rubbish she felt inside. But not this time; this time she knew it wasn't going to end with smiles and laughter.

Coral locked eyes with Aaron and stopped pacing.

"The case of Camilla Bayles," Coral said and gave him a tight smile as Aaron's smile dropped, and so did the glow in his face, all the colour slowly draining away, leaving him to look a greyish tone, sickly one might suggest. This reminded her of Dylan's sickly skin colour, the one he would get from nights spent sniffing line after line of drugs from his coffee table and playing video games till beyond the early hours of the morning.

He ran a hand through his hair and gave a tight smile, regaining his composure but not enough to hide how he had just reacted to Coral mentioning her mum's name. Coral smiled at this.

"Oh, I forgot, you probably hadn't realised I'd figured out that you already knew my mum, once upon a time," Coral said to Aaron sarcastically.

He didn't respond.

"She was beautiful. Blonde, green eyes, to-die-for body, which you already knew, of course. In fact, this was her dress that I'm wearing," Coral said, doing a slow 360-degree spin so he could take it all in, "but you already know that as well, don't you?" she said, smiling at him, thoroughly enjoying watching him shrink away to nothing, taking him down piece by piece.

He didn't respond.

I've got him right where I want him, she thought to herself. He was speechless for the first time, so Coral continued while she had the upper hand. "Her death, well, the police called it suicide; blamed it on her viciously slit wrists and the knife nearby with her DNA on. However, I've always thought differently. She lived life to the full; there was no way she'd give it up so easily, not when she had everything she could have ever dreamt of. Like everyone said, she *loved* life."

Still, Aaron said nothing.

"Anyway, me and my now ex-boyfriend had a very interesting conversation a few evenings ago. He was clearing out the flat he lives in of what the previous owner had left behind. He brought me some trinkets he thought I might like... one of which was a charm bracelet. Now, this wasn't just any bracelet, it was the charm bracelet that my mum used to wear. My dad, every year, on her birthday, would get her a new charm, dedicated to a different country they'd visited or any special memory they had together in a new place. I couldn't understand how it was in the bag of trinkets, but of course, after much investigation, the answer became clear that it was *your* nephew Dylan that gave them to me."

No hint of anything was given away on Aaron's face.

"So this led me to understand that *you* were the previous owner of the flat. There was also the photo that Iris had of you and my mum, an old photograph taken in a bar not from here. You both were looking a lot closer than you should've been. At first, I thought the photograph had been taken years before I was around, but I noticed the bracelet on her wrist and how full of charms it was. So I knew then you'd been the one who assaulted her and caused her to become pregnant."

Coral's skin burned saying this out loud, but she continued, not wanting to lose her moment of confidence. "My brother questioned Dylan further as to what else he had found while clearing out the flat. Turns out he had found a pile of books about the process of pregnancy and parenthood hidden in the bottom of the small wardrobe in the spare room. So, my guesses leaned towards the fact that *you* definitely got my mum pregnant, but she wasn't pregnant when she left this world, so my guesses again go to an abortion, one that she wanted and that you clearly didn't."

Aaron's clenched hands were so tight that you could see his knuckles turning white, just like his nephew's had before. *It seems like this angry streak runs in the family*, Coral thought. His nostrils were flaring every few seconds. Coral stood perfectly still in front of the armchair, arms folded across her chest. "So, you beat up and viciously attacked Iris because she found the photograph of you and my mum, and she and I put two and two together, which can only make me think one thing about the case of my mum. Suicide wasn't involved in her permanent departure. *You* were."

After a few minutes passed, Aaron raised his eyes to meet Coral's and smirked. Coral felt uneasy at the unexpected enjoyment written all over his face of what had just left her mouth; he was supposed to be looking like a deer in headlights as Coral had imagined he would, but he looked quite the opposite. As he pushed himself up and out of the armchair, he slowly clapped his hands together.

"Wow, you *really* did blow my mind with that, Coral. For an artist, you painted a masterpiece. What do you want me to do now? Admit something?"

Coral opened her mouth to speak, but no words would come out.

"You're right about Carena; it was very unfortunate. We were both about to leave the house, and the photo fluttered to the hallway floor from my wallet as I pulled out some receipts. As she bent down to pick it up, she looked it over, and we locked eyes. Everything became a blur after that, but she was about to delve into something she didn't know about or understand; I had to stop her from doing something stupid," he said, smiling calmly.

"By beating the shit out of her? You could've just spoken to her—"

"You know as much as I do, that wouldn't have worked. I had to shut her up; I wasn't aware she'd pocketed and kept the photograph, so I'm assuming she did it as she tried to get away from me. There was no time to think about that, though, as I had to get her to the hospital. Plus, I had to shut you up too, hence why I sent the text off of her phone to you. I couldn't have you both figuring it out, but it clearly landed in your favour anyway. Carena paid the price."

Coral stared at him; she couldn't quite believe what she was hearing.

"Anyway, I'll admit some things to you; I could do that at least. I'll admit that Camilla and I were in love. *Purely*, *deeply* and *truly* in love," every word said from his twisted mouth with great meaning, as if he was trying to hurt Coral verbally. He remained smirking the whole time, clearly enjoying every moment of this. This wasn't the Aaron she'd known all these years; it was like his alter ego.

"She didn't love you; she loved me and my family," Coral started, but Aaron held up a finger, signalling for her to be quiet.

"I'll admit that we went on so many adventures together and never looked back, only forward. I'll admit that she promised me we'd have our own home that we could love and live in together without her having to run off back to her run-down shitty family. When I found out she was pregnant, I was beyond happy and excited. I went out and bought books for her, clothes for her, anything she needed for the pregnancy. She didn't tell me herself, though. I found the pregnancy test in the bathroom bin."

"You're lying," Coral said, "she couldn't have gotten pregnant the night after you assaulted her."

Aaron smirked at this comment. "You're old enough to know about the birds and the bees, Coral, but I'll happily spell it out for you. It wasn't just one night that we made love."

"I don't believe you," she retorted, but Aaron continued.

"Do you know how that made me feel, finding out that she was having *our* baby? I was finally going to have the chance to be a father, the best news I could've ever had, and to a beautiful woman, *my* Camilla," he said, smiling at the photograph on the wall of Coral's mum with Iris and Kruze, the one he'd commented about before.

"She probably didn't tell you because you'd *raped* her, and she was scared," Coral said, making herself cringe after saying the word out loud. The thought of her poor mum being assaulted under his hand was enough to make her want to be sick.

Aaron continued, completely ignoring what she'd said yet again. "I thought she wanted to surprise me in a creative way, wait until she had scan pictures or at least a visible bump. But then one day, she wouldn't return my calls or my texts or anything, which wasn't like her at all. So, I went to her client that she was supposed to be seeing that day and asked him if he had heard from her. He wouldn't tell me much, only that she'd cancelled because she was at an appointment; I assumed it was the hospital. I instantly thought the worst; is Camilla and our baby okay? So I drove up there and was driving around, looking for a space to park up in... I didn't expect to see her walking out of the abortion clinic."

Aaron slowly raised his eyes to look at Coral, which was quite eerie how he did it, a blank look on his face. But he was getting more and more worked up; Coral was certain of that in the silence that filled the room, anger thick in the air from both of them. She didn't want to feel the tension in the room, but it was there, thick enough to cut with a knife, starting to make its way into her head, clouding her thought process. This *wasn't* how she'd expected the conversation to go.

"She didn't expect to see me that day," Aaron continued, moving his gaze from Coral. "She looked horrified to say the least, didn't quite know which way to look. I told her to get in the car so we could go for a drive and talk. So I drove us to a section of the woods near the lake, away from prying eyes, to *talk*. I just wanted to *talk*. The sad part was she wouldn't talk to me. She refused to, but eventually, I convinced her to get out of the car, and we sat on the bonnet. That's when things turned ugly," he said, slowly walking over to the kitchen area.

"What do you mean turned ugly?" Coral asked, knowing full well what was coming. She didn't feel ready to hear the gory details which he was about to let loose out of his sinister mouth. No matter how strong she knew she was, the real truth was going to rock her world all over again; it was on the cards, unfortunately.

"I just wanted to talk to Camilla. She was the love of my life... I just wanted her to *listen* to me," he said, sounding empty, slowly making his way around the kitchen island; every footstep he made had such precision.

"What did you say to her?"

He stopped and placed his hands on the kitchen island work top, his eyes landing on the photograph on the wall once more. "I convinced her to take a walk with me down to the lake, and so we did. We walked down to the lake, and I took her hands in mine and sobbed. I asked her why she had gotten rid of our baby. It wasn't just her choice. It was our fresh start together, and she took it away from me without even considering how I felt."

"What did you do?"

"*I* didn't do anything, Coral. Your mum did. She aborted our baby, my own flesh and blood. I was angry..." he trailed off. "I hadn't been angry in so long, Coral. No one knew what I did. No one knew that I took my anger out on your mum. No one knew that she told me to leave her alone. No one knew that I chased after her as she ran away from me that day."

"You chased her?"

"And then I dragged her to the lake side. That was hard, she put up a fight, but I got a good fistful of her hair," he said, shaking his head. "She was strong, my Camilla. The girl had pure strength in those last moments. I never wanted to hurt her, but she hurt me first, and I was always taught to make things even when I'd been hurt."

"And then what?" Coral asked, her face suddenly feeling wet from tears she wasn't aware had left her eyes; her body beginning to shake uncontrollably.

"I pushed her onto the ground and forced her head into the water. She had to learn how it felt."

"How what felt?" Coral managed to whisper.

Aaron steadily moved his gaze to meet Coral's, his features not changing once. "How it felt to have someone decide whether you live or die."

Sticking her nails into her palms, she tried her best to be calm, but it was becoming more and more of a struggle hearing the words and having them repeat over and over in her head. He did what he did to teach her a lesson. The man who'd spent years living with Luciana and Iris, loving them, bringing goodness into their lives and being the supportive husband and dad to be, was also the man who had torn Coral's mum away from her life, away from Kruze and her dad, ripping their family apart and leaving them to rot away as living corpses, and for what reason? Just because she didn't want a baby she'd been forced to conceive by a selfish excuse for a human.

"You're selfish," she whispered, tears streaming down her face.

"I'm not selfish. We *both* made the baby, therefore we *both* should've had the chance to share our opinions on what happened to it. She should've spoken to me about how she felt before acting on it selfishly. She should've given me a chance to say what I thought and felt about the situation. I didn't want to hurt her. Coral, you must understand that."

"You wrote you were sorry on the flowers at her grave, didn't you?" Coral managed to ask in a shaky voice. Her throat felt tighter and tighter by the second as if she was having an anaphylactic shock attack from his words and the realisation of the horror in her head coming true after all these years, always having suspected the worst but never having the truth there in front of her. But now the truth was out and staring her in the face, she was struggling to open her mind to process it.

How could someone have been so cruel to the angel my mum was when she was on this earth? Coral wondered, her heart completely shattered into tiny shards of sharp uneven pieces, so broken she wasn't sure it could ever be put back together again properly.

Aaron nodded. "I'm sorry for the way it had to end, but surely she knew once she'd had the abortion, without my consent, she'd made a life-changing mistake. She took my baby away... she had to learn the consequences of her actions."

"You're *sick*," Coral blurted out before she could stop herself, losing composure quicker than she wanted to. The words that left Aaron's mouth had left sharp flickers of pain on her heart and her head, her brain feeling as if it was on fire with all the new information it was absorbing, trying its best not to let it in. *The pain is surely going to kill me,* she thought.

"I did what had to be done. I was angry, and she didn't care about what she'd done to me. She never took into consideration *once* about how I felt in the situation. She just chose everything for herself—"

"It was *her* body, that's why," Coral said, anger starting to replace the upset feeling. She would need a few weeks' worth of therapy sessions after hearing all of this. "You raped her and then expected her to keep the baby? She didn't want you in the first place, so why would she want a version of you growing inside of her?"

"What makes you think I raped her?" Aaron asked, a confused expression etching his face. "She *wanted* me; multiple times. Maybe she should've been on a contraceptive pill, and then she might still be alive."

"You assaulted her the night you met her at the bar," Coral spat.

"She came home with me for a coffee after we got talking at the bar and was suddenly in my lap making out with me, and that happened more than once, might I add. I wasn't going to say no, was I? No man in their right mind would," he muttered.

"Fuck you. My mum loved my dad; she wouldn't have given him up for *you*."

"I'll let you think what you want. I know the truth, and that's all that matters. I can take what I did to my grave, and so can you," he said, starting to open drawers eerily slowly. "Working as a detective helped, though. Making it look like suicide was easy enough after the length of time it took for them to find her that day. My conscience began to lift, and I felt free, knowing it was suicide and not murder. Hence why I was able to live again and start afresh. I have no guilt anymore," he said, continuing to look through the drawers. "So, Coral, what do I do now?"

Coral felt her body instantly go cold. "What do you mean?"

"Well, I've just openly told you my secret of five years. I mean, I feel better for telling someone what I did. I know *you'll* feel better overall for finally solving the mystery, but what did you think was seriously going to happen next?"

"I thought you'd turn yourself in and do the right thing, especially because you're so sorry *apparently*," Coral said hopefully.

"You live in a fairy tale, Coral. This is the real world, wake up," he said, pulling out a long sharp knife from the cutlery drawer. "I can't let an eighteen-year-old ruin the life I've made for myself, now can I?" he said, holding the knife up, turning it in the air, admiring it. "That wouldn't be the right thing to do."

Coral reached towards her bra when Aaron pointed the knife at her.

"I wouldn't do that if I were you. Do you think I was born yesterday?"

"I was just—"

191

"I know you were just doing something *stupid*. Let me guess, your phone is tucked away in your bra, recording this whole conversation, and now you want to call the precious police for help. Then what? They'll come and save you, use your recording as evidence so they can arrest me, put me away behind bars till the day I die, and the world will finally be made right again? Is that *seriously* what you thought would happen?"

"I need to go," Coral said, beginning to move in the direction of the front door, but Aaron moved quicker and got in her way, the knife still gripped in his hand, pointed directly at her.

"You really should've thought this through, Coral. I'm disappointed in you; you'd make a pretty shit detective after this hiccup. If you thought that I had murdered your mum, surely you wouldn't have come here alone?"

Coral opened her mouth and then closed it again. She'd let herself into her best friend's house, waited to talk to the man who had murdered her mum, expecting him to turn himself in, and with what backup? Why did she think the man capable of killing someone so easily would happily agree to tell the police what had really happened five years ago? He was a psychopath; of course he wanted to continue his *normal* life with no remorse.

Her thoughts were interrupted by the intense sound of unexpected pounding on the front door, the door handle moving hastily, which sent Coral's heart into overdrive, and clearly Aaron's too with the look on his face. Whoever was on the other side of the door was desperately trying to get in.

17

"You bitch," Aaron whispered, pointing the knife at her. "You told someone—"

"I didn't tell anyone I was coming here," Coral fired back.

Aaron's eyes went so wide as she spoke that she thought they'd pop, and without hesitation, he marched over to her with anger rippling across his face, making her stumble backwards.

"Shut up! You keep quiet, or I'll stick this knife in you quicker than you can blink."

Coral stayed stock-still, her stomach flipping out of control; she was speechless.

"I'm not answering the door, they'll go away, and then we can continue this."

"Continue what exactly?" Coral asked; sweat starting to trickle down her back.

"I said shut up," Aaron barked at her, slapping her across her face in one swift motion.

Coral moved her hand up to her face shakily and jumped as the banging on the door sounded through her ears again. Her cheek burned from where Aaron had slapped her, but she couldn't retaliate. This wide-eyed man before her was capable of so much more than she could begin to imagine. She thought about everything he had just told her, and the words he had said played back in her mind.

I can take what I did to my grave, and so can you, he'd said to her. In that moment, Coral came to a realisation.

I'm never getting out of here alive.

The thought fired itself around her brain like a firework show, shooting and fizzling, smoke engulfing her lungs, forcing her head to spin.

"For goodness sake, who the hell is trying to break down my door?" Aaron sighed, rolling his eyes. He focused his attention back on Coral.

"Tell me who is on the other side of that door, Coral."

Coral's brain had been bombarded so much it had begun to shut down, nothing making sense, everything feeling extremely slow and blurry. All this hard work to find out about her mum had led her to the man capable of taking her away, but not for one moment had she anticipated he would strike again, repeat the past. An eye for an eye makes the whole world blind, but surely not a life for a life?

"Coral... you *need* to tell me," he said, gripping her arms tightly, making her believe the blood would surely stop pumping around her body and her bones would break. "Who the *fuck* is behind that door?"

But again, Coral's mouth wouldn't work.

"Okay, fine... I'm going to go to the door, and I'm going to look through the peephole to see who's clearly got no patience to wait. Don't. Move," he said, pushing her back down into the armchair. "I promise you, Coral. You make a move, and I *will* kill you sooner than I intended, and I *won't* be nice about it."

Coral remained sitting with the sensation of being as heavy as a rock in the armchair, feeling as though she had sat in quick-setting concrete; she knew she wasn't going to be able to get up and out of the armchair with ease again, if at all. She needed to get out of here; no way had she come this far to end up another victim to his bloodthirsty ways. Letting her body do the work as her brain remained unresponsive, she carefully slipped off her heels so as to not make a sound and then placed her feet on either side of them, gripping the sides of the armchair.

If she ran to the sliding doors behind her and tried those, he'd be by her side within seconds of attempting to slide open the door. Running upstairs would be an option, but then where would she go? There was nowhere to hide, and if she jumped out of one of the windows, she'd probably break her leg and not be able to run away from him in time before he'd drag her back into the house to kill her. However, it could potentially give her enough time to ring the police, but what good would that do? By the time they turned up, she could be dead, and he could've deleted all of the evidence off of her phone of their conversation and probably made it look like suicide somehow. If he could do it once, there was every chance he could do it again.

Coral's heart was beating so hard in her chest, she began to believe it would puncture her, breaking through her ribs and revealing itself through her skin. She was sweating from every part of her body, including places she'd never sweat before, causing her to feel hot and clammy, which instantly made her feel sick.

I need you, Mum, she thought to herself, tears starting to blur her vision and burn her eyes. Today was supposed to be the day she got justice for her mum, not the day she left this world to be another murder statistic.

At least I'll be able to see you again, Mum, she thought, her heart breaking over and over again in the seconds that passed by.

For years, all she had wanted to do was die. There was no doubt about it in her mind; the thought of it had been ingrained in there for years, eating away at her, making her plot different ways to end her life every day that passed by. But now, in the days leading up to this, she had begun to realise there was so much she wanted to do with her life. So much time she'd lost in her depression, the world around her black and thick with smoke constantly, the suffocation always taking over.

However, in the time she'd spent trying to find reasons behind why her mum had been forced out of this world, she'd started to let go of the battle-scarred Coral that once was. Yes, the scars would always remain, but she had started to change in such a short space of time. Her roots were starting to show the beautiful blonde she'd been born with, her body had begun to stop craving the feeling of destroying it, and she'd started to focus more on trying to fix herself and the world she lived in rather than destroying it, without even realising it was happening.

As Aaron got to the door and looked through the peephole, he murmured to himself, "I didn't order a takeaway."

Opening the door, with the door chain still fastened, he said, "Sorry, but I didn't order anything. You must have the wrong house, and why are you braying on the door like the world's ending? Did you not see the doorbell? Have you never heard of having patience?"

Coral slowly stood up and tiptoed over to the sliding doors, looking up in just enough time to see the latch was on, but what was on the other side of the door brought tears to her eyes and a flicker of hope within her. She sprung forward the short stretch away from the latch, flicked it so it was off and spun around to hear a loud slamming sound as if the front door had been kicked in.

She inched to the side slightly to see that the door had in fact been kicked in, and Aaron was charging across the room back towards her from the door in what felt like slow motion, knife raised and ready to attack. Behind Aaron, the so-called takeaway man had dropped the pizza box and was running towards him, hands at the ready to grab him with a set of handcuffs gripped in one hand; clearly not your typical delivery man like Aaron had thought.

Spinning her head back to the sliding door, she watched as two blurs of people ran past her towards Aaron. The man behind him lunged forwards, pulling him down to the ground, but not quick enough. As Aaron fell towards the floor, his outstretched arm with the knife in his hand made contact with the first police officer who had run through the sliding door.

Coral let out a strangled scream and called out the police officer's name as her legs buckled and she fell to her knees, hands quivering over her mouth. The police officer with the knife in him and currently bleeding out was Kruze.

18

"It's been three months," Coral started, staring down at the headstone, the old flowers below already having lost their colour completely in the early September sunlight. "I brought the best in the business for you; I know how much you loved these. I'm sorry I haven't been back sooner… I couldn't bring myself to stand here. It doesn't matter how many days pass by… I will always need you here with me."

She leant down and propped the flowers up against the headstone. "Three months is a long time to not come visit; I already feel deep guilt about it, but I know you'll understand my reasons. A lot has changed for me since I came here last. My hair isn't coral-coloured anymore, but I'm sure you'll have noticed that," Coral said, twirling her natural blonde hair between her fingers. "I don't smoke anymore either, and I only drink every now and then, so as you can imagine, my bedroom finally smells fresh as a daisy for once instead of like something's died in there."

Coral smiled to herself. "But something did die in there… reckless, unfortunate Coral did. The old me who took life for granted and wanted nothing more than to be rid of it completely. It took years, but I'm developing into the woman you probably *hoped* I'd become now and the woman I hoped would do you proud."

Looking down at herself and then up into the sky, she noticed the clouds were lazily rolling across the brilliant blue, a picturesque sky that Coral wished she could hold onto and keep in her mind forever. But the truth was, there would be many a sky she would want to hold onto, many a cloud she would wish she could drape herself across, many a sunset and sunrise she would be beyond grateful to still be alive to witness. Months had gone by since the standoff against Aaron, and life had never felt more freeing for Coral; she finally felt alive again.

"I have to go now, and I won't be back for a while... but all for good reasons. You inspired me, and I love you for that," she said, kissing her fingers and placing them on the headstone. "I'll see you real soon. I promise."

Coral collected herself after a few moments of reflection at the headstone and wandered away down the grass, taking in the early morning sunshine and breathing in the fresh cool air. She'd lived and breathed the country air all of her life, never once finding a reason to go off to a city; she was a country girl born and bred, but times were going to be changing, and it was taking a lot for Coral to try to adjust.

After everything that had happened, it had inspired her to pursue something valuable to her life, and after many a rejection, she finally got accepted into a university to complete a degree towards becoming a detective. After years of not getting justice for her mum from anyone, she realised she wanted to do for others what no one did for her. It wouldn't be easy, and it would take more hard work and years of her life than she could even physically or mentally process, but nothing in her life ever had been easy; she was willing to work hard for this. Following in her brother's footsteps would make her feel so accomplished and proud, and she knew he'd be proud of her too.

She looked up as her feet made their way to the truck and clambered in, feeling the smooth leather seat beneath her and breathing in the fresh, clean smell.

"All okay?" Nitis asked, gripping hold tight of Coral's hand and smiling in a comforting way. Coral looked up at him and nodded, giving him her best smile, squeezing his hand back. She still couldn't get used to the fact that she and Nitis had become so close in the previous months, and the support he had given her was enough to make her feel light and airy for a lifetime.

"Thank you for bringing me," she whispered, leaning forward towards him. He met her halfway and kissed her forehead.

"I'll take you anywhere if it brings you happiness," he said in the warmest of tones. He always knew how to make her feel at ease, even in her darkest times.

After things had happened with Aaron, she needed her therapy sessions more than ever, and Nitis had walked her or driven her to every one of those therapy sessions in the last few months. He'd saved up and got himself a second-hand truck, and since doing so, he'd seen Coral every week, whether it be during the day or in the middle of the night. In those cases, she'd creep down the stairs and let him in through the door; he was too good of a person to have to climb through her window. When she was with him, she didn't feel like she had to sneak around; he was the best influence and treated her with the respect and love she'd wanted and deserved for years. In the middle of the night, he would wrap his arms around her and hold her, letting her cry as much as she wanted to or ramble on as much as she needed to; kissing the tears off of her face and replacing them with the warm, fluttery feeling she needed which sent shots of electricity to her heart, making it feel as though it had grown in size.

Coral's happy thought bubble was suddenly interrupted by a painful memory from the past. Aaron had spoken cruel words the day Coral had been brave enough to confront him all those months ago, and they had been some of the most painful words she'd ever had to hear and let absorb into her brain. To this day, she still had no idea if what he had said held any truth or not. Had her mum seen him more than once? Did she say she'd been assaulted as a cover story to have the abortion with lesser guilt than she'd had before? Was her mum really being fully honest throughout the last moments of her life, or had the panic taken over and made her lie to try to keep herself and her family safe?

Coral tried to remember, as Yasmin had told her, that none of that mattered now; it was far into the past, far away from her mind, and she should lock the door on it. Yes, it happened, and yes, it would always haunt her and hurt, and there would definitely be days where she would fall apart when remembering it, but the worst was over with, and that was all that mattered in the long run. Coral couldn't let the past define her anymore; she had to move forward. That was one thing she had learnt with life; it goes on.

Nitis drove them around the village where Coral had grown up before they headed back home, and it was beyond peaceful. Her body felt the vibrations as the calming music tuned into her ears from the media centre, which made Coral relax back in her seat, tranquillity taking over.

She looked out at the houses rolling by and the fields with the sheep happily grazing on the grass, their lives completing the cycle year in, year out, happily achieving what they needed to do; what they were put on this earth to do. Whereas Coral's life had only just started to begin again; she'd completed a great deal of the cycle of what grieving for her mum had done to her, and she was ready to continue the grieving process as well as start again with her life, moving forward into a new territory where she could start to be who she wanted to be. She was heading down a positive road towards her new goals, and she felt strong enough to take on any twists or turns or bumps in the road ahead, knowing she had plenty of support along the way. The pain and loss of her mum would never go away, but at least now she could acknowledge that justice was achieved, and that alone was progress forward for them all.

As they pulled up into the street where her little home was, she didn't feel that pang of pain that she usually felt. She didn't feel the depression suffocate her, the sadness; any of the negative feelings that usually engulfed her didn't this time. Coral just felt light and airy, as if her lungs had been cleared of all the emotional pollution that had been roaming around in there for years; she could finally breathe again, and it felt so good to be able to.

Coral leant over and kissed Nitis on the cheek. "Thank you."

"For what?" he asked, looking at her, that same loving smile always lighting up his face.

"For being you," Coral replied, smiling and leaning in once again, but this time, his pillow-soft lips landed on hers, caressing them, the kiss sending sparks yet again, exploding in both her chest and her mind.

She opened the truck door and hopped out, waiting for Nitis to join her, and when he did, his hand slid into hers perfectly, their fingers intertwining as if they'd once been carved in stone together, always fitting back into the place where they belong.

"Thank you for being you also," he said as they walked up to the front door. "You make my life be what it should be."

Coral opened the door and was greeted with the smell of freshly made pancakes. As she rounded the corner of the wall and stepped into the kitchen, she let go of Nitis's hand and wrapped her arms around the body of the chef making the delicious food.

"You should be resting," she said, waiting for him to leave the chopping of the fruit alone so he would turn around.

"I've been telling him that all morning but it doesn't seem to be what he feels like doing today," Iris said as she walked into the kitchen from the dining room.

"I can rest tomorrow; today, I need to make it special because it's *someone's* last day at home," Kruze said, picking up the spatula and pointing it at Coral, a small smile playing on his lips.

Even though he was beyond proud of her for getting into university and wanted her to succeed in life, he was heartbroken knowing he wouldn't be able to see her every day. The day he was stabbed by Aaron, moments before the homicidal man was swiftly arrested, was one of the most traumatic days for them as a family. Kruze had been rushed into hospital and almost bled out completely, but by some form of a miracle, he survived, but only just. He spent weeks in hospital being treated, building up his strength the best he could, and getting pushed back every time infection hit or the anger of being in hospital and not with his family; even not being at work was frustrating for him.

It was also very hard for him to begin to understand how it had been Aaron, after all these years, who'd taken his mum away from them all, and yet no one had any idea about it. The fact he was a police officer and hadn't sniffed out the psychotic past or present behaviour of the evil man so close to home had utterly destroyed Kruze.

He wasn't one for sitting about, and so recovering from the stab wound was a lot more mentally draining for him than physically. Kruze was beyond a fighter, though, and the week Coral was leaving to go to university was also the week that Kruze had finally been able to go home from hospital. He still had a long way to go, but he'd made exceptional progress in the months that had passed by and had made the most of every second he'd had with his sister.

"Well, you better have made the best pancakes known to be on this earth," Coral said, pinching a blueberry from the bowl of fruit ready to add to the fluffy pancakes on the plate next to it.

"Make the most; you won't get pancakes as good as these for a while."

"Going by your last two burnt attempts, I should think she'd be glad about that," Iris said, smiling and laughing as Kruze threw a nearby tea towel at her.

Seeing Iris smile and laugh brought tears to Coral's eyes. As well as Kruze recovering from the impact of what Aaron did to him, Iris had also had to go through recovery from Aaron's angry outburst attack on her. Iris had lost a great deal in the months gone by, especially her confidence to leave the house, but the lack of confidence meant she couldn't continue with her job. The trauma of being attacked by Aaron, after watching the photograph of him and Coral's mum fall out of his wallet, causing him to attack her and stop her from telling anyone, had left her frightened of the world around her; anyone could hurt her, even the man who supposedly loved her and her mum, and that put fear into her bloodstream and had continued to pump around her body for months, and still did.

She had always pushed aside the topic of men, focusing on her own needs and wants in life instead, and what happened with Aaron had only made her feel worse; all trust gone.

In the last few weeks, she found herself spending more and more time at Coral's house, bringing her mum with her to give her the company she needed. But Luciana was still a mess at what her world had become; it would take her time to be able to do life again properly without suffering every day that she woke up. But of course, it would take her time; who in their right mind could survive after they'd just discovered that their husband-to-be had murdered one of her closest friends years ago and had covered it up for all this time?

Iris had begun working on a business plan with Kruze, and at first it had only been to keep both their minds occupied throughout their trauma. But with their joint knowledge of the ins and outs of business, they soon realised that they actually made a striking team, and she was well on her way to being ready to see a panel and address them with their marketing idea. In the process of working together, it became apparent that there was more than just being business partners between Iris and Kruze, and that was clear to see when one evening Coral walked into his bedroom to find them doing something slightly more intimate than working on the business project together. After days of not knowing how to look either of them in the eye from what she'd witnessed, Coral was just happy that they would at least have each other when she left for university. She didn't want either of them to become lonely and withdrawn, but that definitely wasn't going to be the case.

"Have the pancakes been distributed yet, or do I need to go to the shop and buy some toaster ready ones?" Jayden walked in and said, chuckling to himself as Kruze pulled a face.

Seeing her dad out of his bedroom had become a more than regular occurrence in the past three months, and it was still something Coral was getting used to, but it was a fulfilling thing to get used to. After learning of what had happened to his wife, it crushed him beyond words, and it took him weeks to stop the anger rising in him as well as the tears forming every time he thought of Camilla. Earlier in the week, he'd finally plucked up courage and made an appointment at the barbers, and didn't come home until his hair and beard looked fresh again, instead of looking like someone who didn't own a mirror. Kruze had then taken the opportunity and took his dad out and got him new clothes for his wardrobe, a few shirts and jumpers, and a new guitar to replace the ones that had become broken over the years through the emotional torment he held deep inside.

Jayden also attended therapy sessions for himself with Yasmin over the months gone by, letting out the last five years and more worth of pain and suffering he had bottled up. Yasmin was definitely getting her money's worth from the Bayles family, and Iris and Luciana, but she was helping them more than anyone had in years, providing them with the help and support they needed since recent events as well as the last five years' worth of suffering. It was a blessing in disguise, knowing her little family were taking steps forward to becoming whole again.

* * * *

"It's official; I'm never going to be able to move again," Coral said, lying back on the sofa, holding her stomach. The day had consisted of them all making and eating food, laughing and joking at old photographs, watching old family videos and talking about the future for each of them. It was all Coral had wanted for years, and she finally had it, everyone she loved in one place, smiling and laughing and on the road to recovery. So much time had been spent feeling miserable. But now, it was time for them to all move forwards together and live for the future rather than survive from the past like everlasting wounded soldiers of a war they once fought; they could now wear their medals of honour with pride and put the past they'd survived away on a shelf.

Nitis had offered to help Kruze with the washing up, and Jayden was getting set up, ready to make the evening meal for them all. His speciality: extra filled and crunchy tacos.

Iris happily sauntered into the room as if she hadn't engulfed plate after plate of food and treats all day, causing her to become stuffed like the Christmas turkey Coral currently felt like. She looked at Coral and smiled.

"Well, I sure hope you can move. Get your boots or trainers on; we're going out," she said, holding her hands out ready to lift Coral up from the position she was having her food coma in.

"Where are we going?" she asked, taking her best friend's hands.

Iris pulled Coral up to standing and smiled. "We're going where the road always leads us."

19

As Coral and Iris pulled into the side of the road, the one they were both more than familiar with, Coral's heart began to race. She hadn't been back since finding out about Aaron, and she wasn't quite sure if she was ready to come back here, but it was her last day before moving away; she knew it was better to face it now than in months or years to come.

"I know you haven't been back since... you know. Neither have I," Iris said, stretching her arm out and grabbing hold of Coral's hand. "I just thought, with it being your last day—"

"I know," she replied, giving her a tight smile. "I know I need to face up to this. I need full closure. We both do."

Coral carefully made her way out of the truck and began the descent to the lake. Iris stepped in next to her and grabbed her hand.

"I'm here. I'm right here," Iris whispered, her eyes shiny from the tears forming.

Coral squeezed her best friend's hand and fought back the tears that were beginning to burn her eyes, and they slowly made their way down the dirt path together. The last time she was at the lake, her world had been completely different; she had no idea back then who'd killed her mum or even if her mum had been murdered at all. Being back by the lake, where the ghosts helped fill the hollowness within her, she couldn't help but feel a mixed bag of emotions. All these years, Coral had wanted the lake to give her a feeling of peace, and only now did it feel like it had.

As she took steady steps towards the water's edge, she squeezed her eyes shut and opened them again to let the tears spill and for the sob that built up within her chest to be released to the open air around her. They both sat down, their legs too shaky to stand, and Coral leant forwards, shakily dipping her hands into the water, letting the pain of what her mum went through flood her, feeling the icy cold water on her hands that her mum's body had once been engulfed in. She sat like that until she couldn't cry anymore, until her throat was scratchy and burning and her eyes were puffy.

"I can't do this," Coral said. "How can I do life after all this has happened? How can I go forwards? I want to, but wow, it just seems impossible. *She* never got to go forwards."

"Coral, you *know* you can do this," Iris said, wiping at her own eyes. "You can't let the past determine your future; you've said that yourself. You're better than that. Your mum would want you to live your life, not stay here and dwindle away to nothing because the past has you so tightly gripped."

Coral knew this was true. She'd told herself this so many times in the months that had passed by. She *could* do this, but there was so much that could go wrong, and it frightened her knowing that. The past was the past, but it didn't mean the future was going to be any better. Coral knew, deep down, that she had to try, though; she hadn't come this far to give up now.

Looking out across the water and the treetops above her head, she had a thought.

"People who stand at this water's edge will never understand what happened. People miles away might come here and look at the lake and the village and not know what I had to go through, what any of us had to go through. Especially my mum; they'll never know the suffering she had to go through in this very spot," she said, wrapping her cardigan around herself to keep out the chill of the late afternoon breeze.

"Look behind you," Iris said, motioning with her head for her to turn around.

Coral did, and the weirdest thing happened. Tears started to fall again, but a smile began to spread across her face. She wasn't sure how she'd not seen it, but a bench was behind her to her right, near the water's edge, but not enough for it to be unsafe; a sort of lookout point where anyone could enjoy the scenery before them. It was a beautiful light oak bench, and as Coral edged closer, she noticed a plaque on it.

"Read it out loud," Iris said, once again wiping at her eyes, her freshly cropped layered bob swishing in the breeze.

Coral cleared her throat and nodded. "There is beauty in the lake, as there is beauty in the flowers and trees that surround it. We may have lost a beautiful soul here, but this patch of land gained the soul and added to its beauty even more. Forever loved and forever missed, Camilla Bayles."

A gentle breeze blew through Coral's hair, but the breeze didn't feel cold; it felt comforting. And in that moment, she knew; her mum may have died here, but her soul was still very much alive.

20

Elle climbed the stone steps, the frosty October air nipping at her skin, and knocked on the door; that was the only easy part of this task. Trying to communicate with her son wouldn't be as simple, but when had it ever been? She'd always resented him in a way for blaming her for everything that had happened with their family. At least now, after all these years, she could visit him in his own flat; what a relief it was knowing she didn't have to see her fat lump of an ex-husband sitting in what used to be her favourite armchair in what was once her beautiful home, in order to see her child.

Elle rolled her eyes as her son answered the door with just a shabby looking towel hugging his hips.

"Could you at least put a t-shirt on, for goodness sake, Dylan," Elle said, quickly stepping through the doorway and looking around the living room and kitchen of the flat. Of course, he'd taken after his dad with keeping an untidy home.

"I didn't say you could come in."

"I'm your *mum*; I can do what I want. What took you so long to..." Elle started but then looked her son over. He wasn't damp looking from getting out of the shower; she knew that for sure. "Have you got someone in your bedroom?"

Smirking at his mum, he bit his lip and gazed over to the bedroom door. "Most definitely, but sadly you interrupted the fun we were having."

"Is it Coral?" Elle asked, eyes widening in fear. This wasn't part of her plan.

"God no, I got rid of her months ago and told her I was on it with Becca, and what a delight it's been with her. Curvy girls are my new way of life. Honestly, the way those hips move when she—"

"Dylan, I do *not* need to know the details of your sex life, thank you very much," Elle snapped at him in as much of a hushed tone as she could muster. *Why does my son have so much resemblance of his repulsive dad?* Elle wondered.

Dylan let out somewhat of a cackle and walked over to the coffee table to pick up his half-empty bottle of Jack Daniels. "So, Mum, how does it feel to have a murderous brother?"

Elle shifted from one foot to the other, feeling slightly unsure of where this was going or who could hear them. Dylan took note of this reaction and continued the taunting. "I mean, if I'd been blessed with a brother, and he'd murdered someone so *innocent*, I wouldn't be so confident about it all."

"I didn't know he was going to murder her," Elle said in a monotone voice, a blank expression on her face as if it didn't mean anything, but the look on Dylan's face made it seem that the words were full of something else; something sinister.

"What?" he asked, eyes locking with hers as he lowered the bottle from his lips; the drink was clearly not the most important thing right now for a change. All humour was lost from his face as his jaw went slack, creating an O shape with his lips, a dark hole where self-destruction entered and didn't come back out.

"What do you mean, you didn't know he was going to murder her? You mean... you *knew* about this before *he* did it?"

Elle sighed and grabbed the bottle off her son, taking a long hard chug on the drink, the burn in the back of her throat elating her. That was always her favourite part of drinking alcohol; the burn it gave her, making her feel something different to what she usually felt on a day-to-day basis.

"We need to get rid of Becca first, then I'll explain," Elle said, marching over to the bedroom door. But Dylan was hot on her trail, and he quickly slid in front of her before she could enter.

"Okay, okay, just... go sit down, and I'll get her to leave," he said hurriedly, panic in his eyes.

Elle glared at him and went to sit on the broken sofa, disgust forcing her to sit on the arm so it wouldn't absorb her into it, caking her in the filth it had collected over the years. She didn't want to know about all the substances that lurked on the grotty material.

Dylan slipped into the bedroom, and after five minutes of hushed voices, a sweaty rotund girl with her fringe matted to her forehead, presumably from the heat in the bedroom, emerged from the doorway and rushed through the room with her rucksack clutched tightly to her chest. Just as quickly, she put on her shoes and nervously closed the front door behind her. *Completely different choice of girl compared to Coral,* Elle thought.

Dylan closed the bedroom door behind him and stepped into the living room, this time wearing a long-sleeved jumper and pyjama trousers. He sat himself down onto the opposite arm of the sofa, scratching at his left arm, a habit he clearly had continued since childhood when the anxiety within him made him feel wretched.

"Okay," he said, "as much as I don't want to hear what you're going to say, I need to know."

Elle didn't hesitate; it was as if a great load was getting released off her back as if she'd physically carried the last five years around with her like a mountaineer carrying their rucksack. But there was nothing in her rucksack to help her survive the issues in her life that she was still facing, and she'd known that for a very long time. However, Elle didn't back down very easily, and she was ready to face the challenges ahead and reach the summit no matter how long it would take.

"Your uncle Aaron and I were thick as thieves as children. Always did things together but never got each other in trouble. We were strong enough to take our own blame without needing the blame of the other involved. Once I'd had you at 17, me and your dad married when I was 18, and we chose to move into our own home together as normal married couples did. Aaron remained here in the flat, and it was so hard to comprehend that he wasn't right there with me in case I needed him if my life ever fell apart."

"That's serious separation anxiety, you know," Dylan said, lighting a cigarette.

"We were best friends; when you don't see your best friend every day, it's difficult," Elle retorted, then shook her head and continued. "My life got harder after that; it didn't half fall apart, Dylan. I know your childhood wasn't the best, but I gave you all I could for those 10 years, but you must understand life was tough for me. Your dad slept around with other women behind my back while I was left to look after you and make sure you were okay, like the good mother I was always trying to be, as well as the good wife. I had to remain somewhat sane, Dylan, while your dad fooled around and made me look like a fool to everyone. All the while, I was trying to bring you up practically on my own while still working the job I'd had since 16, and that was painful, more than you'll ever begin to understand."

Elle took another long drink on the bottle and leant her head back, closing her eyes, soaking in her spoken words alongside the comforting burn in the base of her throat. How had her life spiralled out of control so much? How had she become *this* type of woman? If only her family hadn't made the stupid decision to move from France when she was only two years old, then maybe her life could've been so very different. Not perfect, no one's life was perfect, except hers had been once upon a time, too long ago now to remember or feel the joy again; it had completely vanished.

Anger fuelled her again, and she turned to Dylan, passing the bottle his way. She still needed to drive; she couldn't be drunk at her next destination or her plan would go down the plughole.

"I didn't know…" Dylan started, taking a long chug on the bottle, finishing it off completely, right down to the last drop.

"Of course you didn't; I hid it well. But one day, I came home from work to find you in the kitchen by yourself with biscuits all around you at the table, chocolate smudged all over your face and your homework, clearly having the time of your life as a ten-year-old should. Your happiness was what kept me going, Dylan, but that was quickly replaced with the anger I felt from hearing the loud female moans above our heads in *my* bedroom in *my* bed."

The anger suddenly took over, and she kicked out at the coffee table, spilling half of its contents onto the floor; not that it made a difference. It was a shithole to start with; she was only adding to it.

"My anger took over me," she continued, "and so I took all I could find without entering the bedroom and left. I didn't want to leave you, Dylan, especially with that disgusting beast of a father. You were my world, but your dad was foul, and I couldn't be with him any longer and continue the act of his smiling, lucky wife. That's how the world outside our house saw me, and I couldn't stand it for one moment longer, so I filed for divorce and left him."

A long, drawn-out sigh escaped her mouth. Elle had never wanted to admit that to her boy, no matter what, but circumstances had changed, and he deserved the truth.

"If I'd known all that, Mum—"

"What? You'd have resented me less? You'd have loved me more than the sick animal you called *Daddy*? Please, Dylan, save it. I know all of this, but I wasn't dragging you into it. You were a child, you deserved better than that. It's just a shame you had to hate me for all of these years instead of *him*."

Elle slowly rose to her feet and started pacing the room, never giving Dylan eye contact. Cowardly, maybe, but she couldn't let the hurt in his eyes lead her off the trail she was currently on. Dylan leant forward and cleared his throat before speaking.

"I hated him too, you know. He hardly cared for me at all, always telling me to stay downstairs with my headphones in and to not bother him. So I did what I was told. I had no other choice. He should've been castrated as soon as I'd been born," Dylan said, anger lacing his words profoundly.

Elle considered her son's anguish. Too many years had passed to make things right now. He'd learnt to grow up in his own way, maybe not the right way with some aspects of his life, but he'd made some good choices, she hoped. She'd come to terms with it many years ago that re-writing the past was impossible, but that didn't mean she couldn't try to make a fresh start now.

"Anyway," Elle said, trying to focus again, "skip forward a few years, and I'm still working in a job I'm thriving in with a manager who thought my work was brilliant, sharing a flat with Aaron again and being able to live happily and carefree without much pain looming over me... When someone, other than your demonic dad, decided to shake things up for me, but to the extreme this time... I resented her."

"Who are we on about again?" Dylan asked, starting to peel the label off of the bottle still clutched in his hands. "What did this woman do—"

"It doesn't matter what she *did,* Dylan. What matters is she took what was left of a good life of mine, and ripped it in half, then left the broken pieces behind in her wake when she went on to another venture in her life. So I turned to Aaron. I only asked him to break her heart, and therefore she'd lose her family in the process and lose everything like I had... But it got out of hand..." she trailed off, looking around the room, suddenly realising where she was again, the nicotine-stained walls making her feel even more disgusted than she already did.

"Wait… so you asked Uncle Aaron to do what exactly?"

"Well," Elle started, tightening the hair tie she had in her freshly dyed hair, "your uncle is a charming guy, good-looking, probably more good-looking than *her* husband was, so I knew he'd find a way to win her over. He claimed they spent months together, but that was all a lie; it was a few weeks if that. She didn't know I lived in the flat, though; I had to stay in hiding while she was around; we couldn't let our scheme be ruined."

Playing back the memories in her head of what they'd planned made her feel powerful. *It was all working out so well to begin with,* she thought.

"Anyway, they had a one night stand the night they met, then they slept together a few more times; it was only a fleeting romance. However, the last time she did stay over, and once she'd left, I found the positive pregnancy test she'd used in the bathroom bin. The pregnancy test I had kept for *myself* in the bathroom cabinet in case I could… Anyway, never mind, she used it before I could. And before I had a chance to get rid of it, Aaron saw he'd got her pregnant and became obsessed even more with her, obsessed with the idea of getting to have his own little family, which *wasn't* the original plan. But then he tried to call her and she wouldn't answer, so he went to find her, blah blah blah and long story short, things went bad, and well, you know how it ended for *her.*"

"So… because of *your* anger, you involved Aaron… and because of *his* anger, he killed her, which is also from *your* anger?" Dylan asked, looking like the little boy she'd left all those years ago, confusion etching his face more and more.

Elle nodded, so Dylan continued. "And when he got sent down, he didn't mention your name at all, even though you were the cause of it all?"

Elle smiled to herself and then locked eyes with Dylan. "Of course not, like I said, we always took the whole blame if one of us got caught. We'd never grass the other one up, under *any* circumstances."

"Yeah, but you're adults now? Would you have done the same if it had been *you* who'd got caught?"

"Without a doubt," Elle said, but deep down, she was uncertain. She'd had enough hell thrown her way. Would she really want to live out the rest of her days in prison due to someone else's problem that she was trying to help with?

Dylan looked completely dumbfounded; the colour drained from his face completely. She yearned for time with him again throughout his teenage life so she could show him the right path to go down. Elle never wanted this for her son, any of it, but unfortunately, he couldn't change the past, just as Elle couldn't. That was something they'd both have to live with. "Anyway, that's something you keep to yourself, my boy, otherwise—"

"Otherwise, what?" he asked, his eyebrows knitting together, his shoulders automatically pressing backwards in defence. As much as he was trying to be the big hard man, Elle could see straight through him. He was still the little boy, deep down inside, that she'd left behind years ago.

"Otherwise, you'll end up in prison yourself. Don't think I don't know about what things *you've* got up to illegally—"

"How did you know?" he asked, his eyes suddenly stretching to be so big and round she thought they might pop like balloons blown up too much.

"Know what?" she asked.

"Were you watching?"

"What are you talking about? I've got somewhere to be, so can you just explain—"

"I was mad, Mum... really mad; I just wanted some action for my friend. Then Coral stuck her nose in, and now he's probably getting done for sexual harassment. It was so long after it had happened, so it's just pointless charging him now... but if they find out about me, then I'm going away for a while too, Mum... I need to get out of town. Permanently... I need..."

"What did you do?" she calmly asked. Had her son seriously followed in her footsteps without knowing?

"The lesbian we pinned down at the party... Well, when I was walking in the woods one morning, I saw her girlfriend walking through the woods with her dog on her own... I asked her why she'd ratted us out and why her stupid girlfriend had ratted us out, but she was acting as if she had no idea what I was talking about... But no one was around..."

"Dylan..." Elle started but trailed off. She couldn't believe what she was hearing. All this time she thought he'd taken after his dad when deep down, it had always been herself. She didn't want to lose composure, but she felt for him. As a mum, she felt as though she had failed Dylan too many times, and now it had really hit home. She just wanted more for him in this cruel world in which he'd suffered all his life.

"I grabbed her on the wooden bridge when she tried to walk away, and she lost her footing... She would've had me put away, Mum… I don't deserve to get put away… I deserve a good life."

Elle stood dumbfounded. She wanted to help him, hugely help him… but how could she? She'd done bad herself and got let off with it, and now he was in the same situation.

"When I got to her, she looked like she'd been badly beaten, and she was bleeding a lot… If she'd survived, it would've been me in prison, probably for life…"

Elle regained her composure and straightened up. "Everyone serves their time eventually, no matter how many years pass by. Your uncle is a prime example of that. I've already had a life of hell, Dylan; it wouldn't be fair to send your mummy away to be locked up forever without a chance for freedom. I need a fresh start, and this is my one-way ticket to that destination. If you decide you want a change of life too, I can make an input. I'll make sure to get you a good home and a good rehab to get yourself off of the drugs and drink, and I can make sure you're never found out about. Even finding you a good job if that's what you want, with a new identity. Keep all that in mind."

She looked him over, and he looked utterly sickened; he was registering the guilt and the reality of what could happen to him. Elle continued.

"Prison life isn't good for pretty boys like you, sweetheart, just as it isn't good for women like me. As long as you got rid of any evidence, you'll be okay, but I would consider my offer. Anyway," she said, making her way over to the door, "I need to get going. I've got one more pit stop to do. It was really nice finally getting to talk to you about everything, Dylan. Just remember who the bad guys are in this story, okay? I'm not one of them, son," and with that, she closed the door behind her before Dylan could utter another word.

* * * *

Elle walked up the small path to the Bayles' house, taking in a sharp breath of cold air as she used the brass pinecone knocker on the door. She only had one shot at this; there was no room for her to mess it up.

Just as the door began to open, Elle gently tugged on her hair tie until it came loose, and ruffled her freshly cut hair, forgetting just how short it was now, still able to smell the auburn-coloured hair dye around her. She was distracted instantly by her thoughts as the handsome main objective of her mission stood in the doorway, his deep red tartan shirt baggy with a few buttons not fastened, leaving it open slightly, revealing a small sight of his chest. His big blue eyes fixed on Elle's, a small smile appearing on his lips.

"Hi there," he said, looking her up and down in a 'surprised yet pleased with the view' kind of way.

"Hi, you're probably unaware of who I am. I was a friend of your late wife's. I'm Elle," she lied, holding out a relaxed hand, freshly manicured, for him to shake. "It's been a long time since I last saw you, so I wouldn't be surprised if you can't quite remember me."

Jayden stared at the newfound face in front of him, looking amused yet puzzled, but then his face relaxed as he took her hand and gave it one firm shake, a kind smile once again forming on his face.

"I think I vaguely remember your name coming up in conversation. I'm Jayden. Please, do come in; it's freezing outside," Jayden said, moving to one side, gesturing for her to enter. Elle entered the house, sliding past Jayden and slipping off her boots and leather jacket. She then followed the handsome man into the kitchen, already feeling comfortable in his presence.

"Would you like a drink? We've got tea, coffee or wine?"

"I would've had a wine if I wasn't driving, but I'll have a coffee, please, with a splash of milk. No sugar," she said, smiling kindly at Jayden. The kitchen seemed so warm and bright to Elle, the faintest smell of something cooking away in the slow cooker on the worktop. *I could get used to this lifestyle,* she thought.

Jayden pulled out a packet of digestives and tipped the packet upside down slightly until a handful toppled out and fell onto a plate.

"If you'd like to go through to the dining room, I'll bring your drink through." He motioned, nodding in the direction she should go.

Elle made her way through and sat down at the table, and not long after, Jayden followed with a tray. He placed it down on the table, revealing the plate of digestives and both of their hot drinks, steam rising from the mugs, and took a seat facing her. He gave her another warm smile, which sent her mind wandering, and said, "I hope that's good for you. It's been a while since I've made a coffee for someone other than myself, so bear with me if it's not up to your usual standard. I hate to say I'm not the finest barista in the area, so I'll happily make another if needs be."

"It'll be fine, I'm sure," Elle said, reaching for a biscuit to dunk into her coffee.

"So... Elle," Jayden started, clearing his throat, "I... how come you're... I mean—"

"You're wondering why I'm here, and you don't know how to ask that in a polite way?" Elle asked, smiling as she took a small bite of her coffee-soaked biscuit.

"Yeah, pretty much," he said, giving her a sheepish smile and taking a sip of his drink.

"Well, I should've really come to see you when I first heard the news all those years ago, but I couldn't bring myself to do it. You'd just lost your wife; you didn't need me turning up announcing myself to you. Despite all of that, though, I am sorry for your loss. She was a beautiful woman inside and out, and it took its toll on me also when she passed. I literally couldn't believe it," Elle said, looking into Jayden's eyes. *Does he believe me?* she wondered. *Am I being convincing enough?*

"Thank you, I understand that," Jayden said. "I'll be honest with you, for many years, I wasn't in a good place, not being able to justify what had happened and why, and I'm only just starting to get my head around it all and put the past behind me now things have come to light. It's been one hell of a rollercoaster, but I'm getting there bit by bit," Jayden said, his shoulders hunched as he fiddled with a thread on his shirt sleeve, clearly feeling uncomfortable.

She wouldn't settle too long on the negatives of this conversation; she didn't want to make him spiral into a pit of overwhelming gloom again. *I need him to focus on me,* she thought, reminding herself of why she was talking to him in the first place.

"I can only imagine what you've been through. No one should ever have to go through that," she acknowledged, looking down and taking a sip of her coffee. "So, anyway, the reason why I'm here is that

Cammy asked something of me once, and it was a pretty big thing to ask, in my eyes at least. It got me thinking recently that after all these years have passed by, it's even more of a weight on my shoulders that I couldn't really come to terms with, but I knew I had to do it for her."

Elle cupped her hands around her mug, chewing on her bottom lip, proud of herself at the lies she had spun, hoping the next few sentences that came out of her mouth would sound as convincing as she'd hoped they did when she'd practised them to herself at home. She'd come a long way, and this wasn't something she was willing to give up so easily; her lies had to sound convincing. "Hear me out, here, but she asked me to make sure that if anything were to happen to her, at any point in her life, that I would make sure to look out for you, Jayden."

Jayden's hooded eyes lifted up to meet Elle's, his eyebrows ever so slightly knitting together.

"What do you mean look out for me?"

"I'm not sure what she meant by it in detail, but I suppose she meant to just come visit every now and then and make sure you're coping with however she left the world. I know that sounds ridiculous; it did to me too. You've not seen me in years, which is basically like you've never even met me really. Five years have passed, and I had no guts to come here and speak to you, and I wish I had so many years ago, especially knowing you suffered so badly. I feel stupid now saying all of this," Elle said, putting her head in her hands, feeling anything but stupid, the lies tumbling from her lips as if they were gospel.

Jayden reached out and gently put his hand on the table in front of her. "There's no need to feel stupid,

226

Elle. That is a big thing to be asked to do; I'd struggle to know how to go about it myself. At least you had the guts to come here now," he said, giving a gentle laugh to make it a more light-hearted conversation. She looked up from her hands and placed her hand down on the table, close to his but not close enough to make him retreat.

"I suppose so; a little too late, though, I guess."

"Well, not entirely. I know the past is in the past, and that's where I intend to leave it, but you're one of the few people who've actually made the effort to come see me at all during these past few years. Everyone just thinks I'm the depressed grumpy guy that people can't communicate with because I'm a widower. You're the only one who's really tried, even after all these months of me finally going back into the village after years of never leaving the house," Jayden said, slowly sitting back and cupping his hands around his mug, taking a long sip, clearly not caring if it would burn his lips. "It's getting colder outdoors with autumn being in its prime time, so I'm finding leaving the house a struggle really, even though I still force myself to go out; I've always been a summer lover deep down. So, you coming here tonight; it was a good night for me to choose to stay in really."

Elle smiled at him from below her eyelashes, tracing her finger along her lips. "Well, I'm glad I finally made it here and that you can see this as a good thing. I can't imagine anyone not wanting to spend a moment in your company," she said, giving him a knowing smile.

* * * *

Jayden and Elle sat for a while, talking about pathetic things like the weather and village life, making small light jokes that in minutes turned into jokes that tickled them so much, it brought out a laugh in Elle and Jayden that they'd both lost many years ago. It felt good to smile and to see someone smiling alongside her, someone she'd wanted to spend time with for years but couldn't get close to, not being able to think of a way to worm her way into his life. But she'd finally done it, finally planted the seed, and she felt overjoyed inside. *What was I so worried about,* Elle thought, *this has been a piece of cake.*

"You've got such an infectious laugh," Jayden said, beaming at her. The creases in the corners of his eyes may have shown his age, but that didn't diminish the fact he was a very handsome man and spoke with such kindness and humour. All these years, he'd been locked up in this house, collecting dust like the furniture, but now was her chance to dust him off and replenish him again for what he was truly worth; she could make him bloom.

After laughter and more biscuits, Elle peered into her mug after what felt like hours had passed, when in reality it was just over an hour. She noticed the remnants of her coffee in the bottom of the mug and sighed; she'd been here long enough now and needed to leave before things got too suspicious, even though she had the feeling they were past that by now.

Gently pushing her chair back, she rose to her feet. "Well, as much as I would love another mug of coffee, I should really get going," she said, slowly sliding the chair back underneath the table. "You'll be wanting to have your evening meal soon, I'm sure," she said, making her way slowly through the dining room door and out into the hallway to get her boots and jacket back on. Jayden sounded close enough behind her that she could hear his heavy breathing from his sudden movement from the table.

"You could stay for dinner if you wanted; there's plenty for two," he said, placing one hand on the back of his neck, clearly anxious to ask her after years of lacking experience in talking to women. After all, he'd only known her a matter of minutes, really.

How cute, she thought.

"Oh no, I couldn't stay any longer than I already have done. Thank you, though. I do appreciate it," Elle said, carefully slipping her feet back into her boots, dragging the time out as long as she could.

"Well... can I offer you my number at least?" he asked her. Elle raised an eyebrow, and his eyes widened. Jayden began to look flustered. "I just thought... with what you were saying my wife had said to you before about looking out for me; it'd be nice to keep in touch, that's all. You're easy to talk to, and it'd be nice to start up another conversation with you over a coffee again... or maybe wine next time, if that's okay with you, of course?"

"Of course it is, Jayden. I'd very much like to have more conversations with you over mugs of coffee and biscuits, or wine and delicious food, if that's your cooking I can smell," Elle said, giving him a wink and a playful grin while digging into her pocket for her phone. Once they'd swapped numbers and Elle exited the door into the crisp cold evening air, Jayden said something Elle couldn't quite make out.

"Sorry, what was that?" she turned and asked, rubbing her hands together, exaggerating how cold she felt. Deep down, she felt so warm and overly excited, happy-go-lucky like a teenage girl who'd just had her crush talk to her for the first time. It was a feeling she hadn't experienced for many years.

"How did you know Camilla? You never said," he asked.

Elle smiled proudly. "I worked with her in a little flower shop that I own on the outskirts of the village. She might've mentioned me as Daniella, but we decided to shorten our names for easiness at work, you see. So I called her Cammy, and she decided on Elle for me. So I kept that name; it stuck. You can call me Daniella if you like," she said and smiled. "Anyway, thank you again. I'll drop you a text later," she said, turning on the heel of her boot, her smile turning into a devilish one, the sinister look attacking her features as quickly as a leopard attacking a gazelle.

Finally, after years of waiting for her new beginning to spark and a hopeful flame to begin flickering, she felt it was igniting and hoped that it would gradually turn into a roaring fire. *This flower is finally starting to bloom,* Elle thought as she walked away from the house and back towards her car, thinking of the future she had just set into motion. A future that she could feel already beginning to grow and one that she hoped would eventually flourish into something quite promising and beautiful.

About the Author

Sophia Nicole was born in West Yorkshire, and has always had a passion for all things creative. Writing being her first and foremost favourite way to express herself, alongside making music, singing, drawing and painting. She has always loved reading a variation of books, but if there's suspense and a mystery to solve, that's where she's hooked from the get-go, and therefore this is her favourite genre to write about.

Sophia has also always had a passion for teaching young children and has worked in the Early Years sector for over eight years. She takes great delight in teaching the children in her care through creative activities, making sure that their learning is always fun and full of development opportunities.

From as long ago as she can remember, Sophia has always been an 'outdoors girl', finding great delight in getting lost in the woods, exploring a countryside trail, or making her way across a beach, collecting interesting shells and gazing off into the horizon. Sophia finds that being in these environments helps to clear her head and inspire her, especially where writing is involved. And come rain or shine, she will take off on an adventure with her camera, ready to capture all that nature has to offer.

Lightning Source UK Ltd.
Milton Keynes UK
UKHW012040251122
412837UK00006B/469

9 781803 811765